Momma Said, "Hit 'Em Back!"

An Urban Novel Written by

Cynthia Amis Dickerson

In Collaboration with Marian Matthews Nance

Happy reading
Cynthia Dickerson

Cover Photo by - Mrs. Diann Kelley
of Memphis, Tennessee

Momma Said, "Hit 'Em Back!"

By

Cynthia Amis Dickerson

and

Marian Matthews Nance

www.mshbsalvation4me.com

Copyright © 2013

By

Cynthia Amis Dickerson

In Collaboration with

Marian Matthews Nance

1st Edition

ISBN: 978-0-9889887-0-5

Dedications

We would like to first dedicate this book back to God, our Father, who inspired and guided the words on the pages every step of the way. We give thanks to HIM and hope that every reader will experience the power of HIS presence. Without Him none of this would be possible.

Thank you to my family for all of your continued love and support. To my husband Milton Louis Dickerson, my son Milton Amis Dickerson, my step-daughter Kimberly Dickerson, my mother Gladys Hinton Amis, my late father John Edward Amis, my brothers Anthony, Jerry, & Clifton Amis and lastly to my dearest sister Sheliah L. Amis.

- Cynthia Amis Dickerson

Marian dedicates this book to her family: To my husband, Herman Nance, our sons Mario, Andreus, Jeremiah, my beloved mother Verline Mayo, my brothers Larry, Milton, Willie and Darrell Matthews, and to my sisters Doris Matthews and Gwendolyn Matthews Jones.

Contents

Contents

Foreword

Sitting here in the church on the mother's board seat about to witness the most joyous occasion, the marriage of my nephew to such a beautiful girl, I can't help but reflect on his life and how he got to where he is this day.

I was there at the hospital when my sister delivered her second son into the world. He was a scrawny tyke of a boy and only weighed 6 pounds. He had a head full of red hair and the longest little fingers and toes. The baby also had some odd colored eyes, and I wondered, "What side of the family did he get those from?"

When I got the call from somebody named JJ to come to the hospital, I said, "For what?" He told me that my sister was having a baby. I thought, why is he calling me and how did he get my number? Louvenia never had much to do with me. But I guess after all, we are family.

As I look through the clear glass window of the nursery at the baby Johnson name tag, I am proud and yet sad for the little boy lying in the crib. I hope and pray that he turns out a lot better than his big brother or his momma.

She didn't always used to be the way she is, but I guess life has a way of shaking you and turning you into something that you never imagined for yourself. Louvenia was always smarter than me, but her anger often dictated the choices she made in life.

I had more self-control and could think through adversity; whereas, Louvenia was temperamental and compulsive. I always loved her; we were very close in our childhood but as we got older our lives changed and we became total opposites. I tried to understand and reason with her in difficult times but she would only push me away and act as if she hated me.

Foreword

My sister's life paralleled people who have strayed from their Christian upbringing. I loved her and tried to show sincere kindness and not judge or speak to her with a disapproving tone. I also tried to overlook her provocative clothes, abusive language and violent ways. I tried to look beyond her behavior and look toward her heart. On many occasions I had to remove myself from her presence, but my prayers and my telephone calls never stopped. As you begin to read this story, I pray that you will not struggle as I and many in the church often do when it comes to loving unconditionally.

This story will challenge us to take several looks at how we judge others self-righteously by holding them to a standard of our own making-through our own eyes-rather than to a divine standard a-Godly standard where we **all** miss the mark.

There may be someone whom this story will speak directly to. There also may be someone who will totally detest and ignore the very words written on these pages. Oh well, it may not be for you. Then again, it may be *just for you.*

My hope is that each will open his or her heart and mind to the journey that we all must travel and be tolerant and non judgmental of the struggles of people like my sister, Louvenia, and those who often lose their way and stray from the path.

"Judge not, that you be not judged." (Matthew 7:1)

- **Mabel**

1
Momma's Golden Rule

The golden rule around my house and in my neighborhood was, for as long as I can remember, "always fight back." That was the code of the street in Memphis, Tennessee where we grew up. Everybody knew not to mess with Ms. Louvenia and her crazy kids in North Memphis. Momma told me that if somebody hits you even if they just brushed up against you by accident, you pick up a brick, hit 'em or bite the hell out of 'em and make sure you draw gushing blood.

If you didn't follow the code, Momma would beat you with a long, brown extension cord. Just like a horse trainer, drawing her whip, she would draw back as far as she could and land it on your naked back. The beatings were long and hard and felt like she was exposing flesh as she yelled foul, low-down and abusive cuss words. I never could understand why Momma used to beat us so bad. I guess it was because Big Momma, our grandmomma, didn't believe in sparing the rod, but Momma took it to a new and angry level.

Big Momma would discipline in love by talking in a soothing voice and telling you why she was disappointed in your behavior, but Momma didn't care. She was angry, furious and out of control and didn't show no love. Momma stood about 5 feet 5 inches tall, weighed about 166 pounds, with a paper-sack brown complexion and a big black oval shaped mole on her nose. Children used to tease us all the time and say, "Your momma look like a witch—a wicked witch." They were right, because she treated us bad, whupping and cussing us all the time for any and everything.

∽ *Lou's Reflection* ∽

Growing up, I attended Carver Elementary—a mostly black school with a few Caucasian students and African-American and Latino teachers. Attendance was about 1,000 and the classrooms were small and overcrowded.

At one time, the school board threatened to shut the school down because of overcrowding and poor student performance, but the parents rallied together to save the school. There were about 30 students in my class, and Ms. Saunders, my 3rd grade teacher, could hardly keep order. If it wasn't for the little gray-headed, grandmomma-type teaching assistant, we would have run her clean up out of the class.

I remember one time, Ms. Saunders called Momma to set up a meeting because she said I was disrespecting her and disrupting class. Momma came to the school that morning just before lunch-time. That turned out to be one of the most embarrassing days in my life. Momma showed up with some pink, wrinkled up pajamas and some dirty, runned over bunny rabbit house shoes. Her latest wig, one of many wigs that Momma wore, was twisted to the side. She had a 40 ounce of Suds (Momma only drank Blue Label) in her hand. She was there to see Ms. Saunders because I called her a *bitch*. Instead of Momma telling me not to call my teacher names, she walked over to me in front of the whole class and said, "Stop cussing that *bitch* out before I knock the *shit* out of you." To make matters worse, Momma set the beer down on Ms. Saunders' desk, took off her filthy house shoe and hit me dead in the mouth. Then she said, "Yo black ass is gon' get some more when you get home.

You dun lost your damn mind, making me miss my soap operas fooling wit yo ignant ass." She didn't care who was around or where she was when she went off. Ms. Saunders was so shocked that her mouth flew open, her light blue eyes bucked and she did not say one word.

Ms. Saunders was from a private, Catholic school in Boston. Frankly, coming to Carver Elementary School was quite a culture shock, and being in the south was even more of an adjustment. She was a quiet, fair skinned, white woman, thick-waisted with long, pretty, wavy hair. She was always positive and would dish out consequences for abusive language. I really didn't mean to call her a name, but it slipped out before I knew it. I didn't know what the big deal was and wasn't messed up about it, because I heard Momma call all kinds of folks that all the time. Man, I guess that's where I got my razor sharp, rude tongue. I really got it honestly and bad too.

When you lived in Momma's house, you had a choice to make. Either you would be a victim of the pain or you would be the one to serve up the pain.

As I got older, it became easier and easier to serve up the pain. After only a few dozen fights, I really enjoyed seeing the fear in their eyes and the spouting of fire red blood oozing from torn black skin.

∾ *Lou's Reflection* ∾

Holding on to the iron bar, I grip hard remembering how I got the scar above my right eye. I was in the park near the projects we lived in at the time. The sun was shining yellow bright, the wind felt good as I twirled around in a circle with the other kids on the merry-go-round. I really liked the merry-go-round because it was just the right size and would go real fast. The swings, the monkey bars and the slide were too big for me to climb on, so I didn't like those.

One day on the playground-I was still in diapers, so I must have been about three years old-John John, who was 5

years old, wanted my spot on the merry-go round. I told him naw, and I didn't move. He pushed me hard to the ground and took my spot. When I fell, my face hit a broken beer bottle laying in the dirt. Warm blood drizzled down my cheek.
 I ran to the house, and Shunkendra and Ray Ray, two neighborhood kids who were in the park with us, were running right behind me. They told Momma what happened and why my face was bloody. Everyone in the house, Momma and all my brothers and sisters spilled out running at breakneck speed to "whup" some *ass*.

By the time Momma and the rest of the family got to the playground, Ms. Ophelia was already there because she witnessed the fight from where she was standing on her porch. She was really angry because she watched her kids and didn't believe in nobody touching them. Ms. Ophelia was a widow whose husband died in the Vietnam War. She worked as a cook at the corner grocery store because she didn't believe in welfare and handouts. I guess she had too much pride. She said she could take care of her own kids. After all she had more children in the neighborhood than anybody.

I remember hitting John John with my fist over and over again. I could hear Momma screaming, telling me not to stop hitting that fool. Then I heard Ms. Ophelia say, "Please don't kill my baby!" When she jumped in to stop the fight, Momma grabbed a hand full of her hair, slung her to the ground and started kicking her.

Momma just wouldn't stop kicking and stomping Ms. Ophelia. When Ms. Ophelia cried out, the rest of her children ran over to block Momma from further hurting their mom. The kids were shouting, "Get off, get off her please." Then, my brothers and sisters jumped in. It was on then! Just like a wrestling match, WWF at its finest. Before we knew it, it seemed like everybody in the neighborhood had joined in the fight. That's when we heard the sirens coming and the "po po" showed up. I looked up, the park had turned dark and the crowd had scattered, but my family was still fighting. Since Ms. Ophelia and her children were bloody and had lots of bruises, we were the only ones put in the police "paddy wagon" that night.

Dealing with the police was something that happened "erry" day, "all day" at our house and in the hood. We were proud to take a ride to the police station that night. Not only was it expected, it was our rite of passage. If the whole family took a ride with the "po po," that kind of rep told the folks in the neighborhood not to mess with those "ignant" fools.

2
Raw Justice

It's time for dinner and I got ta get my head right. My street guard has to be up. My walk, my talk, everything about me has to be hard, and I can't show no sign of fear. Male testosterone has a sour, thick, funky "in your face" odor. The sour smell lingers in the air. It makes me long for a time when I was in the company of any one of the many female friends I screwed around with.

It's 1992, I'm twenty-two years old and I've been in this place for two years. This prison just outside of Jackson, Tennessee is a hard place. It changes you from an already bitter person into an even more callous and hard-core animal. I am far away from everyone I know, and it's like my whole world has disappeared. I walk around numb and feeling out of step. It feels like someone else's life is unfolding right before my very eyes.

How did I get to this God forsaken place? My life, my world has spun out of control, and all I can do is sit here trying to figure out what went wrong.

ॐ ॐ

Laquita Green was my girl, cute in the face, slender and fine. She was 16 and I was 15; I liked dating an older girl. She had the greatest legs-the kind that could wrap around my entire back. She would put on high-heeled shoes and the sight of her would make my knees buckle.

Smart and a straight "A" student, Quita came from a home with a momma and a pops. They would "sweat" her all the time with strict rules that left her hungry for more exciting fun and adventure.

She craved and loved the thug life. She loved for me to flash my shiny grill. Quita was the kind of female that got a thrill from committing petty, dangerous crimes. Our relationship was like an addictive drug to her. She loved the fact that I looked different from most of the cats that lived in her neck of the woods. My long, shoulder length locks intrigued her, and my slender, 6'4" muscular frame really turned her on. Quita would often say my light-brown eyes were sexy, and she felt like I was undressing her with them. When I was aroused, they would get lighter and change colors, showing I was ready to get my groove on.

Laquita's eyes would brighten the same way and she would tremble with joy in anticipation of the pleasure of being a part of my world — a world of dark, violent and corrupt pursuits.

One day after we had been hanging out at the pool hall, Quita said she was bored and tired of shooting pool. She suggested that we go do something fun. After we had walked a couple of blocks, she saw an old, frail, white woman walking with a wooden cane and a straw bag that was swaying in the wind. The plan was for Quita to walk up swiftly to the vic strike up a conversation, and then I would rip the purse from the "vic's" hands.

We would run in two different directions and meet in the alley after five minutes. Quita didn't care nothin' bout the money, just the mere satisfaction of taking the purse, the horrified look on the woman's face and the high pitch sound of terror after the snatch and run. This time we got caught.

Quita's father, Mr. Green, had money. He owned two fine food restaurants, really elegant places and her Pop's best friend was a local, high-profile lawyer. He's the one that posted Quita's bail the same day, and she was released. She only got a lecture from the judge.

I never saw Quita any more. Her parents forbid her to have any contact with me. After all, to let them tell it, it was my fault that she caught a case. But if they only knew that their sweet little baby girl was the main instigator. I, on the other hand, was not so lucky. I got an overworked, inexperienced public defender. First of all, he was late, and then he fumbled through his briefcase and stuttered the whole time while talking to the judge. Billy Weinberg was his name. Ain't that nothin! This guy looked like he had never seen the inside of a courtroom. His clothes were outdated. He had coffee stains on his tie, and his pants and jacket didn't match. He had on some patent leather shoes. Not only were his shoes patent leather, they were scuffed and muddy like he had just come up out of the woods. I thought those shoes went out in the 70's during the disco-fever era. At one time I thought he was gonna get up on the table and break out into "the jerk," one of Momma's favorite dances back in the day. He looked a "hot mess."

The courtroom was packed. I thought they would never call my docket number. The bailiff was a big, muscle-bound joker—looked like he should be in the Mr. World competition. He had a jacked up attitude, but didn't nobody give him a bit of trouble. When the judge finally got to my case, he didn't look very happy. He had an awful scowl on his face. Judge Oscar Pettigrew was his name. Pettigrew "The Shrew" is what they called him.

As we approached the bench, I learned I had been charged with petty theft. When Mr. Weinberg started to talk, he was so nervous and was stuttering so bad that the judge couldn't understand what he was saying. Judge Pettigrew got so irritated that he talked directly to me instead of directing his questions to my lawyer. After about 3 or 4 minutes of questioning me, Judge Pettigrew told me that the old lady whose purse we snatched didn't press charges, which was why he was letting me off with a lighter sentence. He ended up sentencing me to 2-years probation and one year of community service. He told me he never wanted to see me back in his courtroom or any other courtroom again. If he saw me again, it would be a much different story.

I guess it's true, you get as much justice as you can pay for. Quita only got a slap on the wrist, but hell I got a sentence. Man, I didn't have a chance with the defense I had. A po', broke ass brother from the ghetto gets no justice, no justice at all.

3
The Straight-Laced Life

My Momma, Louvenia Johnson, only worked a job for two months at a time. Just long enough to get food stamps and welfare and satisfy her case worker who would visit four times a year. Momma would do most any and every thing to provide a crib, food and hand-me-down clothes for us kids. I got so tired of wearing other folk's ugly ass clothes I didn't know what to do.

Kids at school used to tease us because we used to wear tee shirts from white, private schools and churches on the other side of town. Everybody knew that our Momma didn't know nothing 'bout them white folks at those schools. Even with all of Momma's gigs, hustles and government money, she still just couldn't make ends meet.

My old man, Jack Johnson, better known as JJ, was in and out of our life. Momma would let him come and go like a revolving door. Other times, he would be living with his latest alcoholic or drug addicted old lady. Drinking and smoking was a habit he kept and wouldn't let go. Momma had a love/hate thing with my father. He would sweet talk his way back in our lives over and over again.

J. J. was a tall, bony, hard-rocked face dude, with locks that hung below his shoulders. He was a half-decent man when he had a clear head. The only thing is, that didn't happen that often. Like me, his rep meant everything it dictated every choice he made in life. My pops cussed everybody out and talked crazy to anybody, just like Momma. Each incident almost always ended in a knock-down, drag-out fight.

So many in my life lived a corrupt lifestyle, but one guy in the neighborhood, Paul Paul really stood out. He was a straight-up gangsta, the kind of guy that would "kite" checks, pimp women and bootleg videos, music and CD's. He would fence jewelry, auto parts and cars. You name it, if it could be "got," Paul Paul was the man to get it. Most all of the kids in the neighborhood, including me, wanted to be like Paul Paul because he always had cash money and lots of it. He had one of the best houses in the "hood." It sat on five acres of green, grass land with big trees and beautiful flowers. The house was gated with armed guards, and you would always see expensive cars and limousines pulling in and out of the big wrought iron gates. Can you imagine, a big, fine house like that—smack dab in the middle of the ghetto? Who would have thought that he would give all of that up? But that's just what he did. All of a sudden, he changed. For real though, no jive. He sold everything he had—all his worldly possessions—and gave the money to different charities. He actually walked away from his beautiful home, his fancy cars and all the "bling" and moved into a run-down rooming house. He just started to be good on the real side with no more slip ups.

The whole hood kept trying to peep his card, waiting for the slip up to be seen and waiting for the hustle to be read. We could not believe Dude was for real. He walked around the hood like he didn't care people were checking or jiving him. He started carrying books and going to that stupid Vocational School, talkin' bout he gon' get his GED. Givin' money he didn't even have to that gheri curl, shiny suit wearin, whoremongerin', lying ass, pimp-daddy preacher.

He was always talkin' bout being saved. I said, "Saved from what?" I don't know what happened to that brother in that "Holy Roller" Church. Did he mean saved from all that bad ass sangin' and raisin' hands and praise "bull?" Making all that damn noise and just goin' on and on and on, singin' the chorus ten, fifteen times. It just don't take all that in those "stay beggin'" for yo' money churches. I didn't understand the guy. He said he was what you call "celibate." Talkin' 'bout he ain't gon' touch no woman until he get married. That fool had all kinda fine women runnin' after him. I believe he got hold of some bad weed—turnin' all soft and sweet like some damn cotton candy.

Yeah, that Paul Paul was some kinda straight-up arrow brother, and even though I didn't quite understand why he did what he did, he reminded me a lot of my Aunt Mabel. I guess I thought he was a lot like her, because she didn't live a corrupt life.

 ❧ ❧

My Aunt Mabel was Momma's baby sister. She was very pretty and really smart. Behind her back, we called her a grown up nerd. My Aunt Mabel read one book a week, the local newspaper and two out-of-town newspapers everyday. She graduated from high school her junior year and earned a scholarship to attend a local college. Momma said she refused to go to City College and went to some college up north cause she was shame of her family. Me and Momma barely finished high school. My grandmomma dropped out of school in the 11th grade to marry my grandpa; that's why years later, Grandma was proud when she earned her GED.

Aunt Mabel went off to college and finished in three years. She never called or wrote the whole time she was at school. When she came home, we found out she had married her college sweetheart, Winton Pruitt.

Mabel was 5'9" with long, beautiful legs. She wore her

hair in a short afro cropped to her head. She wore dresses and pants that usually had tops and bottoms to match. She was a Bible School teacher, and from time to time, she was a guest speaker at different churches around town. Momma didn't like her talking that preachin' talk around her or her children. Momma didn't never have nothin' good to say about her sister. Not only did she call her a holy roller, she used to call her Ms. Goody-two shoes.

She used to say Aunt Mabel thought she was better than the rest of the family because she had two little ol' degrees, a lousy husband, a house and kept driving new cars. Aunt Mabel tried to be nice, but Momma wasn't nice. She would sometimes invite Momma to her house to meet some of her friends, but Momma never would go.

Momma would always say she didn't want to be bothered with those ol' uppity stuck up Negroes. Aunt Mabel would even buy Momma stuff when she would go shopping, but Momma was still mean to her all the time.

Momma's sister had a big house with a nice front yard and a big back yard with swings and a gym set for her two boys. Her house was so big that her two boys, Carlos and Carlton, had rooms of their own.

They were one year apart, but they looked like twins. The two boys never got into confrontations with other children. They seemed to have a knack for staying out of trouble.

My cousins had oak furniture in their rooms, and their navy blue and tan covers on the bed matched the curtains. The windows would swing open to the outside, and each window had a screen on it. In the summertime, you could open the windows, and the flies wouldn't even come in. They used to open the window for fun in the summer because they had air that came out of vents. They didn't have no window fans or air conditioners sitting in the window blocking the outside view.

Aunt Mabel and Uncle Winton were married for 30 years and they seemed happy, like folks on TV. Uncle Winton was shorter than Aunt Mabel and was chubby. The rare times I was allowed to go over to their house, I saw how they had certain times for everything they did. They had times to get up, cleanup, study, (even if you don't have no homework. That's crazy!) Times to eat together, devotion time, play time, inside time. Even when it's still daylight, my cousins had to come in the house. Man, I couldn't and didn't want to live like them. Momma would say all the time her sister was raising her boys like girls. Mabel's boys went away to college and graduated with honors, and they have good jobs. They both are married and have families and each of them has a son and a daughter.

4
School Daze

Three more years have passed, and it's 1995. Sitting in this cold, gray cell, I can think of people to blame, or I can blame myself. I wanted to be cool or seem like I was cool in everything I did. That's the way I wanted to be seen. I never made a perfect score or even came close on a test in school, cause I didn't want that kind of rep. I never answered questions, even though I knew the answer and could correct the teacher. I hated the smart kids—they were lame and stale. Their conversation was whack, and their clothes were jacked up. I didn't want to be like those "nerdy" kids, but I wished I coulda found a way to be smart and cool.

I wished I had tried a little harder in school—to be a semi-serious student. Maybe I would have if Momma had encouraged me just a little bit. Momma didn't even know when the six-week's report cards came out, let alone whether I had C's, D's or *F's*. Heck, I even had to sign my own card. Life might have been a little different for me. Who coulda stepped to me and rapped about how I could be cool and yet still be a good student? I really can't put all the blame on Momma. I realize that some stuff **you** have to take responsibility for, and encouraging yourself is one of 'em.

❧ ❧

My 8th grade art teacher, Mr. Stennis, was very creative. He was what you would call a "free spirit." He was a little weird too, but he really knew art. Mr. Stennis was a tall, lanky man about 6'2". He wore wrinkled clothes all the time, and was not very fashionable, but he was cool. He was the kinda "cat" that always wore a hat. You would never see Mr. Stennis' hair, at least the top part of his hair anyway. Maybe he didn't have much hair in the top. He sported a beard and side burns and horn-rimmed glasses, which he never wore. It wasn't nothing to see Stennis with his glasses tucked into his shirt pocket or sitting on top of his hat. He was an okay looking guy, but most of the female teachers stayed away from him because he didn't engage in a lot of chit chat. He was more interested in his students. No one ever missed his class. I think it was because he gave us a lot of freedom and let us do some really crazy stuff, all in the name of self-expression.

There were really no limits to the art projects we could create. He challenged me to be myself and not worry about being cool, smart or anything; however, I couldn't bring myself to be that kind of student in any of my academic classes. In Mr. Stennis' class, we didn't have tests, there was no competition and all the work was based on individual creativity. If the teachers had been more like Mr. Stennis, and if I had been more willing to lay down my rep, maybe I wouldn't have done some of the same dumb things that my brother, Tae, did. He was smart too, and he never lived up to his full potential either.

My oldest brother, Martavius was killed in a drive-by shooting when he was only twenty years old. He had been in a gang since he was twelve. He idolized the gang; it was the close knit family he never had. He had a kind of kinship he would have given his life for—and that's exactly what happened to him. He was shot thirty times in the car; the carpet and seats were so soaked with blood that it looked like a wild animal had been slaughtered. No one in the family could bear to look at the car.

Momma lost her joy, and her will to live after that. Each day she died slowly, she was never happy again. That's when Momma started drinking and drugging. Momma would get up in the morning drankin' and smokin' dope. She loved to fight. She would pick fights and taught us to do the same.

Tae was the oldest boy and Momma always treated him different from the rest of us. It was because she really loved his daddy, Big Tae. He was nothing like my Pops. Momma and Big Tae met in high school. He was 17, an all-star football player, about to graduate with lots of college scholarship offers. When Momma got pregnant with Tae at 16, she never told nobody—not even Big Tae. Maybe she didn't want to mess up his chances of getting out of the ghetto and doing something big with his life. As time went on, I don't know why Momma never told Big Tae about his son. After all, he was a "big time," pro, stand-out player in the NFL and was banked up.

Momma let Tae do whatever he wanted. She would give him money. He never had to do any chores around the house, and she let him stay out late and not even come home some nights. He would just be hanging with his boys, and hanging with his boys is what got Tae killed.

I remember me and Momma standing at the graveside as Aunt Mabel finished singing "Amazing Grace." Momma hunched me in the side and said, "Didn't nobody tell that cow to sang, she always trying to run something. She gets on my last nerve, uhhh, she's a piece of work." I told Momma, "Don't be like that. She's just trying to help ease the pain." Momma looked and scowled at me, and just before she could get a cuss out, the preacher interrupted with prayer.

The day we buried Tae was a beautiful, cool, sunshiny day, and after hearing the song and the prayer, I felt comforted. The calmed feeling didn't last as the sound of the casket being lowered into the ground brought me back to reality. I guess it's because I knew that was it. I would never, ever see my big bro' again.

When I looked around, I didn't see none of his "so called" homies, the ones he called family. They didn't even show up to pay their last respects. I thought it kinda strange that none of his boys were there when he died, and not a single one came to the funeral or even to the gravesite.

We always wondered who killed Tae. Whoever did it, we wanted the killers dead. We didn't care who it was. We just wanted revenge. Some blood had to be spilled for the murder of my brother. We had to let a few years pass so we wouldn't be suspected of the brutal killing, but somebody was going to have "hell to pay" for taking my brother out.

5
Vengeance Is Mine

Rage is what I feel most of the time. I'm mad at Momma because she was irresponsible and didn't take care of us. I'm angry at my Pops because he was a deadbeat. I'm angry at them fools that killed my brother, Tae, because they was supposed to be his partners. I'm angry at Quita because she influenced me to do the wrong thing. This must be why I can't seem to be happy for very long. In prison you can't show any sign of weakness or softness. If you do, they'll think you a gal. I gotta live hard, and if I gotta die—I gotta **die** hard. I don't know no other way. I was raised to take from a sucker and beat his face in if he tried to stop me. Anger, vile language and beat-downs is what I am about, and if you try to punk me, your damn life is mine.

It's Sunday, and Momma's comin' to see me. During visits, we talk about times before I came to this hole. She gives me the low down about all the niggas in the hood. The whole scoop on who slangin', who shackin', who wheelin' and dealin.' We talk about the family and how she struggling to make due. She tells me the S.O.S.—same old shit—every week, same old stories just a different twist and spin on the same old lies.

Momma lookin' old, hard, and smoked out. She had me at 18, and now at 44 she look mo' like she dun lived half a century.

I'm 26 years old, and I'm facing a long prison time. As I watch Momma, her mouth is moving, and I notice thick, nasty, yellow, slimy snot running from her nose.

Momma spits in my face and her voice gets louder and mo' ghetto with every word. The female guard comes over and tells her she gon' have to leave if she don't hold it down. "I know she ain't talking to me," Momma say as she rolls her eyes and looks the guard up and down. Moms gathers her purse and says, "I know she don't want me to go off up in here. Bye, cause this heifer don't want me to catch no case up in this hell hole." I watch her staggering and mumbling to herself. As she leaves, she passes the guard, rolling her eyes again and tossing her head in the air. The same scene's gonna play out next week when she comes to visit one mo' gin.

As I walk back down the narrow hallway to my cell, I see Sarge. I turn the corner, and he's looking creepy and watching me as I walk to my cell. He comes toward me looking me up and down with his cold, greedy eyes resting on my joy-stick. He takes his night-stick and slightly taps my shoulder. He then asks me in a high pitch voice if I need anything. I have to watch my step because this "perv" is just looking to send me to the hole. Once there, I been told the guards will rape you and make a whore out of you for days on end. I am a young buck.

My last AIDS test came back negative, so I'm safe for now. I give this fool a hard stare and say, "Main, I'm good!" I step off and walk swiftly to my cell. As I slide to the back wall of the cell, I make sure I don't lie down or sit on the bed.

Sergeant Whitaker slowly walks and drags the top of his night-stick across the bars of my cell as he wags his filthy tongue at me.

As he passes, I imagine visually killin' that sick S.O.B. plastering his blood all over the floor and walls. I would jerk that long, skinny stick out of his hand and pound his head with all my force and strength until you could see the white meat. I could see my mouth gripping and twisting as my eyes bulged and every muscle in my right arm strained to inflict pain. Just as my hand went in the air to deliver the fatal blow, I hear the Preacher Man, singing "Doctor Watts"—an old familiar hymn that my great-grandmomma used to sing with soulful gospel emotions.

Three hours pass and I awake to the ringing sound of the dinner bell. As the cell door opens, I walk to chow with Preacher Man. He is a chunky, bright-skin man that looks a lot younger than his forty years. He has a gheri curl, a full beard with pork chop sideburns, and he's been to seminary. I believe him when he said that he's been to seminary, because he's very intelligent, and when he speaks about the Bible, it sound like it's true and he knows what he's talking about. He's in the joint because he lost his temper in a heated church meeting and beat-down one of his deacons really bad.

The Chairman of the Deacon board accused Preacher Man of stealing money. The church meeting was called because the two men were accusing each other of stealing money, and they were arguing among themselves. The deacon had been stealing money for years, and Preacher Man had proof that he was going to present to the church. So, when the Deacon heard through the grapevine what Preacher Man was gon' do, he passed around some damaging pictures of the Preacher Man showing him in a less than favorable light. The pictures had been altered with another man's body attached to the Preacher Man's head. During the meeting, the deacon stepped to the preacher and put his finger in his face. The deacon hit the pastor several times. There was a scuffle and the deacon was beaten severely. He suffered broken limbs and multiple cuts and bruises.

"Vengeance Is Mine"

As Preacher Man shared the story with me, I could tell that he was still very angry about the incident and he had not forgiven the man. True, Preacher Man was defending himself, but he continued to hit the deacon over and over again slamming him up against the brick wall in the basement of the church. Even when the deacon lay bleeding on the floor, no one even tried to break up the fight. I don't go to church, but I can't see nobody whupping somebody in the church house, and still calling himself a preacher. I know I have pent-up rage, but looks like Preacher Man got me beat bad. To this day, the deacon is confined to a wheel chair, and Preacher Man accepts no responsibility for the part he played.

I ask him, "Why can't you forgive the deacon?" He replies, "I didn't do anything, he framed and attacked me." Finally, I say to Preacher Man, "Excuse me if I'm wrong, but does God look at who started the fight or does He look at the hearts of both you and the deacon? God forgives us for the wrong things we do, aren't we supposed to forgive others when they do us wrong?"

I wonder why the Preacher Man won't answer my question—why he just walks away from the table and goes to sit down with four other inmates as if I hadn't said a word to him.

I look over at him as he sits and engages in conversation. He is a different kind of person, odd and peculiar. I want to know how a man of God can do something like that and not see his part in the fight? Even though a wrong had been done to him, how can he not see his own offense? Aren't we supposed to forgive others when they do us wrong?

After talking to Preacher Man, I can see how unforgiveness has affected him and made him into a bitter person. I know I have bitterness and rage, and I have obsessed over killing the perps that killed Tae, but my rage is small-time compared to Preacher Man. He let his whole church down when he didn't handle the situation with the deacon well. Instead of threatening to expose the deacon before the church body, he should have first met with the deacon and a couple of the elders in a private meeting to try and resolve the issue of the missing money. Maybe then the two of them wouldn't have gotten into a fight, and he wouldn't be in jail. Man, how can he be so blind? For a man who has read and preached the Bible, I can see that, and I ain't never even picked up the Bible. This is too much for me to wrap my head around, so I might as well eat this bad ass food.

I eat the dry beans, the mystery meat, the hard string beans and the burnt bread. You either eat this garbage, or you go hungry. I choose to eat this smelly slop.

6
Stand Your Ground

Prison life is the worst kind of life. You have to constantly watch your back. You have to watch the fool inmates, and you have to watch these salad tossing, peanut butter packing, bribe taking prison guards, too. The kind of dudes that come in here are hardcore. They street fools who take what's yours in a slick and conniving way. They physically and aggressively take from you what they want. Living around mean guys like this makes you hard and unfeeling. When you let your guard down, you can lose your life, or worse, your manhood. For me, I wasn't going out without a hell of a fight and I was gon' make damn sho' I wasn't nobody's bitch.

If you showed any sign of being soft, yo' bootie would git took. "Man up" was the name of the game in this hell hole. I've seen so many come in here and just give in because they so scared—scared to stand up. The way to survive your time in here is to be crazy and be willing to die in a brutal fight if someone messes with you. The kind of fight that was bloody and very violent with kicking and beating and hardcore rage. It was times like this where the code of the street came in handy. I had a lot of experience from all those neighborhood fights.

I had been locked up for only a little while. I knew some scumbag punk was gon' try me to see if he could make me be a gal. What they didn't know was, I was waiting on some fool to make his move.

I was in the yard. It was sweltering hot and I was just

hangin'. Some of the guys were shooting hoops on the court, another group was playing dominoes and in another corner of the yard, some had a game of spades going. "Rec" time was a special time that everybody enjoyed because we could get some sun and those that liked to work out could pump some iron and flex their muscles. Me, Preacher Man, Riguez and some of the guys I thought was pretty cool were just sitting at one of the wooden picnic tables and observing everything.

A basketball rolled near the table where we were sitting, so I stood up and walked toward the court to throw it back to the guys hoopin'. A big, ashy, freckle-face, six foot four inch inmate with red locks, fronted me. They called that rascal, Scarlet.

Scarlet was the kind of brother that would try everybody that came to the prison. His main M.O. was intimidation. He would try to get his bluff in early, and if you fell for it, it was all downhill from there. Scarlet said, "It's time Main, you can make it hard or you can make it easy, but you gon' be mine."

Before he could say another word, I 'bust' him in his mouth. I grabbed his locks and with all the force I could muster, I kicked him in his lower jewels. When he doubled over, I threw his body against the cement wall. He screamed, "you son of a bitch." Before he could get it out, I clamped my teeth down on his ear and spit a piece of the ear on the ground. I kept punching on his lifeless body until the guard dragged me off. The last thing I said to that punk was, "You really pissed me off—you must don't know who I am. I'm from Norff Memphis and I'll kill you, you freckle face ass hole. I deal with bullies like you all the time. All mouth and can't fight your way outta paper bag."

One of the worst things about prison is you can't trust no one, and there's always some fool that wanna prove that he can control you—who believe that sex with a man is different if you just want to relieve yourself, and you don't attach any emotion to it. It's like a girl that say, she a virgin, but she won't think twice before she let somebody eat her out.

The attempted booty-taking scene with Scarlet wasn't the last time I had to fight, but it doesn't even compare with this. As three of the punk-ass prison guards jump me and slam me to the floor with bone-breaking force, I realize this is one ass kicking I just gotta take. It's all a part of the game just to prove to everybody that I ain't no punk and they got to "bring it."

Sargeant Whitaker and the other guards take turns hitting me and kicking me. I try to cover my face, but my mug keeps getting' hit over and over. A door opens up and I hear voices. I try to hold my screams, and the next thing I know, I am in a dark, narrow room.

7
Out of the Darkness

I am stripped down to my underwear. I'm cold, I'm sore and don't feel nothin'. I'm not angry, I ain't scared, and I'm not depressed—I feel absolutely nothing.

The silence is different though. I don't believe I've ever experienced this type of solitude. I try to recollect when I have ever been alone with no noise. I realize for the first time that I really don't like to be by myself. Why have I never been alone with me? Am I that bad? Do I like me? I hate myself. I never ever knew that about me. I need to get out of here. I bang on the door screaming for someone to let me out. My hands are sweating. I drag my hands across my 'draws' and I realize that there are open wounds. Did I get them from the guards beating me, or did I get them from banging on the door? For the first time I realize that the guards did not get the chance to violate me.

I hear someone breathing in the corner. The room is very narrow, and it's pitch dark. There's no can, and no bed, and man, I want out. I hear breathing again. Is it a person, or is it my imagination?

Am I losing my mind? I'm so scared to be alone that I'm hearing things. I just want to end it all. I want to die right now. It's so dark in here, and yet I feel like someone's in here with me. Who is it?

I listen closely. I can hear faint breaths being taken. I ask, like a fool, "Who's in this room with me?" No answer. After about two minutes, a quiet, baritone voice says, "You are not crazy. I'm in here with you."

"Who are you? What's your name? How did you get in here?" My voice cracks as I tremble with uncontrollable fear. "Louvious Latrell Johnson, don't be afraid," a faint voice whispers. The voice calling my whole name comes from the far right corner. I'm not a spiritual person, but for the first time in all of my life, I pray to my great-grandmomma's GOD. "Lord, I have never asked for anything, but please come into my life. I can't bear to continue to live like this. I don't want to be scared and sad anymore. I believe your son, Jesus, came to save a 'fool like me.' Please forgive me of my sins." Instantly, I began to feel a peace I have never experienced.

Just when I feel like I'm floating, I hear the quiet voice again, "I am Gabe, and I am here to save you from the depths of hell. On more than one occasion, you wanted to end your life. Let's go back to the two times you wanted to end it all. Do you remember sitting in your cell with Rodriguez? You were feeling hopeless and very depressed."

ॐ ॐ

I remember that day well because Rodriguez was taking a dump in the already foul unbearable funky odor. I was already at a low place, and he really irritated me. That was the point I started calling him "Stinky Riguez." He was always stinking up the place with his burrito, taco, black bean, cheese on top eating ass. He's 5'4" slender and covered in tattoos, from Tijuana, Mexico. At least twice a month, we had a taste of Mexico and Italy flava', and on those days, he really got his grub on and who paid for it, but me. When I got on him about eating all that greasy stuff, he would get teed off and start rattling off Spanish words really fast. I knew he was cussing me and calling me all kinda names, so I told that fool that if he didn't speak English, it was gon' be some sad singing and flower bringing, and his family wasn't gon' never know what happened to his stankin' ass.

I wonder how different my life would be if I had not followed in my Pop's footsteps. Would I be sitting here now thinking about ending it all just so the pain would go away? It would be so easy. Nobody would care anyway. My momma, pops and my family don't give a damn about my existence so why should I. Even stinky Riguez, in the cell with me right now, don't give a damn.

My life is so screwed up. If I took my head and rammed it against this thick wall until I lost consciousness, would Riguez stop me? Would he even care?

As I sit here thinking about ending it all, I can't believe all the triflin', evil, things I've done in such a short time. If I kill myself today, will I go straight to hell? I wonder how and if I can change? Is there any hope for me?

"Do you remember asking those questions on that dark, depressing day, Louvious? God loves you and you have taken the first step to salvation." God told me to tell you. "You must go and speak for me"

"Do you remember another time when you almost died when one of your friends held a gun to your head? You and some of the guys were behind a vacant house shooting dice, and you were bragging about being on a winning streak. You had won about $100 from them, and you were talking too much about nothing—just running your mouth, when Ben pulled a gun from his pants leg and threatened to kill you. He drew his gun so fast it took you by surprise. He pistol whupped you and put the gun directly on your left temple and pulled the trigger twice. The gun jammed twice, so Ben punched you in the face."

"You kept saying to him, "Kill me, I'm ready to die. Go ahead take me out of my misery." You were spared that night, Lou, and all the other times you talked about killing yourself. Today, you need to turn your heart over to Christ.

God loves you and he's offering you grace and mercy. What will you do now? It does not matter that you are locked up. You need to use your voice to spread the good news. God told me to tell you, 'You must go and speak for Him.' God saved you in order for you to save others, and he wants you to start with Paul Brown."

"I don't know who that is." "You will know in due time. From this moment on, you must be a new creature in Christ."

Suddenly, the door to "the hole" opens. The guard tells me that the guys that touched me inappropriately had been fired, and that I'm free to go to my cell. As I walk to my cell, I pass Preacher Man's cell and hear the guard call his name, "Paul Brown, your attorney is here to see you." So, that's Paul Brown! Well, I'll be damn. Ain't that some shit! Oops, forgive me, Lord, I'm trying to be a new creature.

8
Say It Ain't So

It's Saturday morning, and I can hardly believe it's 1998, and I've been here eight long years. I notice it's really quiet on the cell block, and usually stillness means something is gettin' ready to go down. I feel like something is about to happen and it ain't gon' be good. If I was at home, my senses would be on full alert, but for some strange reason, I feel serene and composed.

I have never felt this kind of emotion for any extended period of time, not even in my dreams or even when I was sky-high on dope. I have had a lot of time to take in all that has happened to me in the last few days. Lord, what is different? Oh, whoa, I'm not agitated. I feel, well, happy for no apparent reason. Is this how you supposed to feel?

Today is visiting day and Momma is coming to see me. I wonder how she's going to take the news about me being saved after being in prison eight, long years. "Lord, *please* don't abandon me now." She has never trusted the police or stealin' preachers. How can I tell her my calling is to preach the Word?

The guard is calling the list of people who have visitors. My name is called. I am nervous, my armpits are sweaty and dripping with moisture, but surprisingly, I am straight.

Momma is wearing a tight, black and white print dress with loud pink colors in it with some black, high-heeled shoes and an ankle bracelet. The dress is two sizes too little, her boobs are exposed—as usual—, and the dress is too short for a woman her age. I never know how long or what color her hair is going to be. This time her wig has blonde and brown streaks in it and comes down to the middle of her back. She has long, thick eyelashes that look extremely fake, and some equally long and luxurious six-inch finger nails.

Momma has what looks like about 2 or 3 colored and brass bracelets on each arm that clang when she walks. I notice Momma's got an extra bulge around her waist, but I guess I never noticed it that much, because Momma dresses this way all the time. But now, I see her differently through the eyes of a man that has been converted. She looks much older than her age with all that makeup and the bright pink lipstick that matches her outfit. Wow! Momma is really not that old, but she looks older and she acts like a teen. I love her because she's Moms, but Momma looks a "hot mess!"

"Hey son, what's shaking? I had to come again to show all these folks how your Momma roll. They don't know nothin bout me in this joint, especially that woman guard. She just 'J.' Always staring at all of this," as she gestures towards the length of her body with her hands."

"Hey, Momma, I'm fine," I finally say as I stare at her "getup." "Son, you don't look right, what's up?" "What makes you think something's wrong?" "I know you, Pimpin," Momma says.

"Momma, I have changed." "Wait," she interrupts, "What kind of change?" "I turned my life over to Christ." "What the hell is wrong with you? The hell you say. You come in here, and fool, you dun turned on me. You know you wasn't raised like that. Naw, naw, naw, Hell naw, I ain't gon' let you go out like that, you damn fool."

Tears roll down her face, making deep trenches in her thick makeup—too light for her skin. She is quite angry. I closely watch her mouth, but I don't hear the words. I knew this was going to be difficult, but I can't believe she is this angry! I have never seen Momma this pissed off before, not even when I got in trouble.

"You dun' come in here and got all soft, dumb and stupid. What you doin' up in this hell hole? Are you giving it up, dropping soap? I would rather you do that than to be turned out like this. What will people say? Main, say you playing, say it, say it! You bringing shame on our family," she says as she closes her eyes. Then she tightens her fists in the air and cries, "I feel like someone dun' sucker punched me in the gut."

"I need to get the hell out of here. I feel sick. I come to see you, and you dun' messed up my high. You better fix this, make it right, or I'm never coming back."

She moves close to my face. I see the "off color" makeup and smell the cheap wine and the weed. In the past, I would have felt the urge to get high, but not this time. Wow! It doesn't phase me what my Momma thinks. She looks in my eyes, and she knows she has lost. She storms out screaming, "Outta here, outta here!"
I stand there watching the woman who gave birth to me. How can she be so upset with my new-found transformation?

She's part of the reason why I am sitting in jail. She told me to steal so many different kinds of merchandise from so many department stores that they called me the "home-boy shopping network." I stole, destroyed property, keyed cars and busted folks in the face for her. I guess this new conversion of mine won't keep me committing criminal activity on demand for her.

It's funny, I don't feel unhappy or sad that she reacted the way she did. Momma is going to have to deal with my new way of life. I won't let her dictate my actions any more. I will only be directed by the Word and my Lord. Wow! I can't believe a heathen like me is actually thinking these kinds of thoughts and these types of words are really coming out of my mouth. I feel so sorry for my Momma. Her personal flunkey has changed his life forever.

The guard walks me back to my cell. I feel so weird. I

feel like a total stranger. I don't know if this new person will be able to hold this lifestyle together.

An hour has passed, and it's time to eat. *"You need to talk to Paul Brown!"* Hey, that's my voice, but how did that sentence creep into my thoughts? How can my voice tell me to talk to Preacher Man? Is this God speaking to me? Oh, I know, I'm supposed to witness to him. This is something I will have to learn to do. I've got to listen to my voice even when I don't generate the thought and know that it is God speaking to me.

9
Forgive & Restore

Dinner time in the joint is very subdued. Everybody is hunched over their plate and not a lot of talking is going on, at least not until they're finished eating their slop.

I'm sitting at a table surrounded by eight other men dressed in denim shirts and jeans with their booking numbers printed in black on the front left-hand side of their shirts. The metal plates on the table contain brown beans, cornbread and a stiff, dark colored meat. Metal cups full of warm water sit next to each plate.

Preacher Man enters the Chow Hall and gets his food. He walks over to another table, avoiding me. From across the room, Lou calls to Preacher Man, What's up?" As he sets his tray on the table, Preacher Man stares me down, still steaming from our last conversation.

Lou says, "Hey man if I did or said something to offend you, God is my witness, I'm truly sorry." As he turns his nose up at me, Preacher Man says, "Dude, when you start putting God in your sentences?" Preacher Man then picks his tray up and walks over to my table.

"Hey, man I want to talk to you about what happened to me when I was in the hole."
Peacher Man asks, "How did you get out so soon?"

"First, let me tell you the whole story and then I need to talk to you about forgiveness."

"Let me stop you right now, Lou." "You can talk to me about anything you want, but I don't want to hear nothing about no freakin' forgiveness. We had that discussion before."

Lou says, "Alright Man. But first hear me out! The guards beat me really bad. I was thrown in the hole without any medical attention. I was not about to let Sarge violate me and try to take my manhood without a fight. When I tried to defend myself, two guards jumped me and threw me in the hole. Man, it was a miracle that they didn't get to abuse me. After that horrible beating I experienced, I wanted to die. I felt so empty, so alone, so desperate to feel anything—anything other than how I was feeling. I wanted to check outta here. No one would really care anyway, because I didn't. I was really in a bad place. I remember my great grandmomma praying, and I cried out to God to help me. At that very moment, I was not alone. I had a person to visit me in the hole. I know, I know, you think I am either crazy or I'm lying. I know I sound like a deranged person running off at the mouth, but I can attest that this is the truth, so help me God."

"Look, Lou Man, are you sure you didn't have too many blows to the head?" "Man, I think my Momma thought the same thing too. When I told her yesterday that I got saved, she got so angry she said she was never going to come back to see me again.

I'm telling you man, I'm not crazy. The person who came to visit me in the hole said his name was Gabe." "What did you say his name was?"

"He told me as plain as I am talking to you. He told me his name was Gabe."

Preacher Man leaned in, "Then what happened?"

"He knew all about the repulsive things I had done in my past."

"Hey, what's up with the new dialogue? What gives man? Every word that used to come out of your mouth was slang and now your whole vocabulary is different."

"I have changed, Preacher Man. That's what I'm trying to tell you. My old self—well, it has literally disappeared. I can't explain it. I can't put it in words. Any way, this person is walking me through my life. I see my life unfolding right before me. Look, it is not a pretty sight, but Gabe tells me I am not alone—that God loves me. He even tells me that God wants me to speak for him. Can you believe—a person like me, with all my priors?"

"Lou, man, this is some deep stuff. Dude, you been called to serve the Lord." "Have mercy, I guess I have," Lou sighs.

"Now Preacher Man, I know you don't want to talk about this, but I think you need to hear me out about the subject of forgiveness. I know you are angry. You feel like God has forsaken you, but you must forgive that deacon at your church." Preacher Man protests, "You don't know anything about my situation. You weren't there, that man started the whole thing. He lied on me and tried to ruin my reputation.

He tried to turn my congregation against me when he knew he was the one stealing. And to make matters worse, he was passing those distorted pictures around for everybody to see. And you want me to forgive him, somebody I trusted? I was trying to do the right thing by defending myself, and it got out of hand when he hit me. He made me do it. It was all his fault. I never would have touched him if he hadn't laid his hands on me first."

Lou replies, "I hear all of that, Man, and what you're saying is true, but still what I **do** know is that forgiving is not an option. If you want to move on, you first must forgive. After Lou says that, Preacher Man pauses for a long time and it was as if God himself was speaking. "Wow!" He exclaims. "How many times have I told that to someone? I get it, Hmm, I really get it. I receive it. I hear you talking, and that message is for me."

The bell rings, and it's time to return to the cell. Neither one of us has touched our food. I tell Preacher Man, "Let's continue this topic at another time."

A week goes by before I talk to Preacher Man again. I see him as I'm walking to Sunday church services. We find two seats in the back. Five middle-age women come without fail to the prison to teach the word and sing inspirational "old school" gospel.

The last time I attended the service was two years ago. I came only to get out of my cell. I moved close to the front because I just wanted to see some young, sexy females; instead, I saw some older women. Their dresses covered their shoes, and they didn't have on any makeup. That turned me off, so I didn't bother coming back.

This time I sit in the back, but the whole scene is different. The ladies' attire is exactly the same as two years ago, but this time they seem tranquil and angelic. Their words are so profound and overpowering that tears rush down from my face. At first I thought it was sweat pouring from my forehead. Then, I believed my sinuses were draining and my eyes were watering. Finally, it hits me. I am crying—the hardcore me is crying like a toddler. This is strange and so intense. I can't believe I don't feel ashamed. The new sensation of crying is so restorative, so redeeming and healing to the very core of my existence. I am experiencing something new in my life where it feels like the shell of the old me is slipping away.

I believe I am undergoing some sort of alteration. It is scary and at the same time I am enjoying this new modification. I am weeping, and I feel the presence of the Holy Spirit in the room. I feel calmed, loved and a security that I never felt even with my own mother. It is the same feeling I felt in the hole that day when I surrendered to Jesus.

It is very different now. I am in the midst of my fellow prisoners, and I don't care how others think for the first time in my life. I love this new emotion, and it makes me feel a kind of euphoria that is addictive in a good way. I really feel happy. I hear every word the female preacher so eloquently articulates. The gospel folds out like a musical composition that no rap song can match. I can sit and hear the message for hours. When the message ends and the preacher gives the invitation to come to Christ, suddenly, I am up front. My tears are flowing and I can't control them. The ladies instantly are comforting, touching and consoling me.

This scene is so overwhelming that I feel like I am about to pass out. The lady preacher puts some oil on my forehead. I feel restored and she then prays for me. This kind of excitement is too intense not to praise God, and I can't be silent any longer. I scream out, "Thank you, Jesus!" so loud that it scares me.

I find myself raising my hands and just waving them in the air uncontrollably. I keep shouting over and over again, "Thank you, Lord!" It's scary, but I don't care. This must be my calling. I was given a Bible, and I was told to read the good book every day.

10
Disclosure

The next day while walking outside on the yard, I see Preacher Man. He approaches me with a curious look on his face. "Mr. Louvious Johnson, I watched you during the church services on yesterday, and I have never observed a parishioner participate in church with such passionate involvement in all my life. You were so connected that it seemed as if you were the only person feeling the presence of the Lord. I tried to focus on the minister's sermon, but I could not focus for watching your actions.

"Lou says, I had never experienced the wonderful, peaceful, calm expression of shared love in a religious ceremony. I did not want the service to end. I enjoyed it just that much!"

Preacher Man interrupts me and says, "I hate to change the subject, Dude, but you know why **I'm** here in jail, but what I want to know is, what did **you** do to end up in this place?" "Do you really want to know what crime I was accused of?" "Yes I do, I want to know how you arrived at this prison?"

"My story started when I was reckless and had unprotected sex with my girlfriend, Sheree. We had a beautiful, chocolate bundle of love. One night we were just kickin' it and having fun like we do every night. The house was full of people and I had been drinking and smoking blunts all day. I was so high—I don't even have any memory of that night.

My five month old baby girl died in her baby seat, and I don't know how it happened. I was accused of her death, because I was the only person to change her diaper and give her a bottle that night. I racked my brain everyday for weeks after it happened and I still can't remember.

There was no evidence, no proof or even any testimony that indicated I was guilty, but I was convicted anyway. I know I am a lot of things, Preacher Man, but I AM NOT A KILLER AND I KNOW THAT I COULD NEVER HURT MY CHILD! NEVER!"

"Man, that's a sad story. I am so sorry for your loss. I can't see you hurting anyone either. Maybe the truth will come out someday."

The guard came over and told us and the large group nearby to split up because he thought I was getting too rowdy. He directed me to the far left of the yard and told Preacher Man to go to the other end. As I stared at the open field, I realized that whenever I shared my story, I felt rage and extreme agitation. This time, I felt slightly agitated, but in a calm way. I feel so relieved. Thank you, Lord!

11
The Secret Is Out

I can't believe four years have actually passed since I had a visitor. Sheree is certainly the last person I expected to see. All these years, I thought she hated me and blamed me for the death of our baby, and here she is standing in front of me with snacks and something to drink. Momma would always bring me snacks, so it was nice to have a treat again from someone other than her.

She looks like she did over a decade ago. Seeing her after all these years, I think she looks amazing! She looks prettier and her skin is flawless. But, why is she here and what does she want from me? I can't believe that this tall, cinnamon brown woman that happens to be the mother of my dead child is here to see me.

∾ ∾

We met in the juke joint club. Several guys approached her to talk to her, but she rejected them.

Sheree was a pretty girl, and I really don't know why she let a fool like me into her life. We became very close, really quickly. Several days later we were intimate. The next thing I knew, she became distant. Later, her girlfriend told me she was carrying my baby. I asked her why she would keep something like this a secret? She told me she wanted a baby so she could leave her mother's house. She said, "This baby is not about you at all. We don't need you in our lives." I felt used, because she had it all planned out without consulting me. She didn't care. She wanted to get free housing and receive public assistance. Wow! She used me and was going to use the baby to live apart from her mother and me.

I was furious, but I played along so the two of them could be a part of my life. Once she began to show, her appetite for getting high increased and the frequency doubled. I tried to convince her that this behavior was not good for our unborn baby. She told me to mind my own damn business. I was distressed when she wouldn't listen. I just could not change her mind. I fell in the same drug trap. We were only kids, but at 18, we had a baby and were playing around with our whole lives ahead of us. Little did we know we were headed for disaster.

∽ ∽

Now Sheree sits in front of me with tears in her eyes, looking sad beyond belief. She says, "I have something awful to tell you, Lou." I wonder what could be more terrible than your infant child dying? With tears in her eyes, Sheree says, "You didn't do it, you did nothing wrong." I ask, "What are you talking about?"

"We were all high that night, but you were more high than anyone in the house. I didn't tell you, but our baby had congestive heart disease. The prosecutor knew about her diagnosis, and he told me not to say a word. He threatened to send my mother to jail for selling drugs and passing bad checks."

Sheree hesitantly continued as the tears plopped on the front of her blouse, "My mother was killed last night. I can't continue to have you rot in prison for something you didn't do. My life is a mess, and I got to make this right today. Baby, I am so sorry. I have known the truth from the beginning. I was not honest with you, but I can't deceive you any longer. I'm sorry, Lou. I'm so sorry."

I sit in silence. My body droops in the chair, and my head begins to throb. I play the words over and over in my head. I was framed by my girl and the prosecutor. This can't be true. I search her face for the joke that is being played on me. For the first time, I realize that Sheree is sober and has just admitted the horrible wrong that she perpetrated against me.

"What does this mean?" She cries, "You are innocent and I will work hard to get you out of here. I have already contacted an attorney to represent the case. He assured me that your civil rights were violated. It will take some time, but he can help to exonerate you." This news was so shocking; it sounded like something straight off the worst episode of a crime show on television. "Are you telling me that you sacrificed my life so that your mother wouldn't go to jail?" "I'm so sorry, Lou." Can you ever forgive me? "Pleeease forgive me." She sobs uncontrollably, "My Momma's dead. My child is dead and I can't continue this lie."

I could not breathe or focus on what was happening around me. I couldn't feel any kind of emotion. It felt like I was on something, but it was all natural. I sit there unable to feel my arms or legs. Suddenly, the pain is so unbearable that my heart feels like it might split in two. I sit without saying a word until the guard announces that visiting hours are over. The last thing I hear Sheree say is, "Are you going to be all right?" I say nothing as I watch her leave the visiting area.

It's taken me about a month to process everything that Sheree told me about how I was framed for the death of our baby.

12
Deliverance

As I lay here on the cot in my cell, I remember how precious my baby girl, Lourita, was. Lu Lu was my pride and joy, and I never thought I could miss anyone as much as I miss her—the smell of her hair and her tiny little hands and feet. Her skin was so soft and she always smelled like baby powder. She had the sweetest smile and her eyes were exactly like mine. They would light up and change colors when she was happy. It is such a relief to know that I did not kill my baby. I loved her so much and, deep in my soul, I knew that I couldn't have harmed my sweet little darling Lu Lu.

I never will forget the time I read *Goldilocks and the Three Little Bears*. It was the three of us—me, Sheree and little Lu Lu. The baby was sitting on my lap and Sheree was there on the couch near me with her head close to my lap. The lights were dim, and as I read the story, Lu Lu was cooing and making her baby sounds. I noticed the shadow of our reflection on the wall and felt sooo happy. For that brief moment, we were a family, and it felt really good because I was basking in the scene and thinking how this feeling was better than any kind of drug or alcohol I could take. Having the memory of that one precious experience is what kept me from losing my mind and ending it all.

Wow! It's almost impossible to believe that Sheree, who put me here, is working to get me released. Knowing that I am innocent just about blows my mind. The police and the prosecutor looked the other way when the evidence pointed to my innocence.

Even though I have committed criminal acts in the past, I did not deserve this prison time. "Lord, you are going to have to help me forgive. You must give me a double dose of forgiveness for Sheree. I can't believe I'm still struggling with this, especially after I preached to Paul Brown about forgiving the deacon. I see now that forgiveness is not that easy. It is a difficult process and is easier said than done. She conceived that beautiful, precious infant, and she let me carry the burden of thinking I was a cold, heartless baby killer for years. I almost took my life several times and I harbored so much rage and aggression, I can't believe I am still standing."

Tears and a sense of liberation are released from my life this day. I fall to my knees, folding my body in a tight ball. I cry, "Lord, have mercy on me! I'm in agony in this jail cell and I need you to help me right now!" The sound is loud, like a wounded animal being attacked. The cell block was always noisy, but the shrieking, high pitch sound shut down every utterance. I am crying and one by one I hear crying like dominoes echoing through the cell block.

"Lord, have mercy on me!" "Lord, have mercy on me!" "Lord, have mercy on me!" It sounds like men being tortured. No, it sounds like a musical interlude of men crying out to the Father. Wow! This experience is such a release. It's like an intense explosion—an eruption of agony and deep deliverance. It is worth every second of every year of hard time I have endured. This is pure, unashamed worship and men are calling on God to come into their lives. I now know that I have a calling on my life, and that I was sentenced to bring about this spiritually enlightening moment. I repeat the words just a little louder, and I hear the words being spoken again and again, over and over. The words get louder and louder and weeping and words sing out in the atmosphere. The words begin and end, begin and end, starting a melody of spiritual declaration that speaks to every one's soul. I am so immensely happy that I cannot contain my body or emotions.

For several hours gospel songs filled the atmosphere, and I can't remember feeling such contentment ever in my life. As the different voices continue to ring out, a familiar song plays in my ear. I remember now, it was a song by Dr. Leo Davis "God is Able." This song helped me endure some of my hardest trials in prison. I say loudly, "Thank you Jesus".

13
Free at Last!

I was ecstatic to see how God moved on the cell block that night. When I went down on my knees, who could have guessed that God would touch more than fifty men and they would give their lives to Christ in such a spiritual way.

My case has been up for review for 3 ½ years and it's now the end of 2001. No one wants to take ownership of the mistake of my wrongful imprisonment. Everyone is blaming each other. How can the courts take this long to release me when they know I was framed? No one cares that I am still in jail, despite all the evidence proving my innocence. I'm not worried, though. I'm at peace, because I know God is in control.

Finally, on Saturday, June 29, 2005, fifteen years since the day I walked in this place, I am in my cell reading my Bible when the guard says, "It's all over man. You're free." I search his eyes and look in his soul and I can't breathe. Slowly, tears begin to fill my eyes. It seems as if time stands still and I am afraid to repeat the words the guard spoke to me. I stare blankly at nothing. My mind is just blank. The guard excitedly shouts, "Did you hear me, Johnson pack your stuff, it's time to break camp!" I drop to my knees, and then lie prostrate in front of the Bible that has fallen on the floor. I praise God, think about my great grandmomma and begin to sing, "What a joy, what a fellowship, leaning on the everlasting Arm."

On the next day, Sunday, June 30, 2005 at 9:30 am, I walk out of the prison a free man. I harbor no ill feelings toward any man, because I am truly a new creature in Christ. As the city bus approaches the curb outside the prison, I notice many family members coming to visit their loved ones incarcerated behind the twelve-foot fence. It is a familiar sight, one that I know I will never miss. I pray for each one of them as they proceed down the steps and pass me single file walking to the entrance of the front gate.

I step on the bus, and the bus driver cases me up and down wondering what I am waiting on. I ask, "How much is it, sir?" He tells me, three dollars and I drop the fare in the box. Then, I carefully put the two dollars and a single twenty-dollar bill back in my pocket—money given to me upon my release from a long 15-year journey of confinement.

I hesitate on whether to sit up front close to the driver or in the back of the bus. I decide to sit in the last seat on the back row. When the bus pulls off, I never look back. I can hardly believe this day is really here.

Looking out the window at all the trees and farm-land with the various crops and animals, it's so amazing how much you miss the simple things in life. Seeing all the different, luxury ranch-style houses, some with pools and even tennis courts was really something to see. I really expected to see the same barns and small wood-frame houses with tin roofs as I did coming to the prison, but now most of what I see is acres and acres of land with white picket fences and sprawling manicured landscapes. To see how this area has progressed from small farmers to rich land owners—Wow! How things have changed.

As the bus approaches the city, I notice that the houses are closer together. The traffic has picked up and the noise levels are elevated with horns honking, lots of cars moving about and many people walking up and down the street. There are a lot of boarded-up houses and I see guys hovering as they sit on milk crates on empty lots, loitering and drinking out of brown paper bags. I see people sitting and standing around makeshift tables playing dominoes and card games on what looks like wooden doors that they have probably taken from some of the abandoned houses. As I glimpsed, I notice that they are doors because I see the shiny door knobs on the bottom and the topside.

I round another corner, then I see guys in hard hats working at construction sites and the smoke stacks from the local manufacturing company fill the air. That's unusual, when did companies start working people on the Lord's day? I guess I have been gone a long time. Things sure have changed. Even though I don't recognize some of the new sights and sounds, they are very familiar and I know that I'm getting close to home. Man, it sure is good to be free from prison! As I look at my watch, I notice it's 11:00 am, and I realize I don't know where to get off the bus. I got so caught up in being free and watching the scenery during the ride that I really hadn't thought about where I would go. I can't go to Momma's house, so maybe I'll go to church.

14
Answered Prayer

I get off the bus down the street from the church I used to attend every now and then just for the food and fun youth activities. I hear the piano and the organ bellowing out the good old gospel notes. I walk up the church steps of New Christian Holiness Tabernacle Church. The soloist is singing, "I turned my life over to you, Lord." The Pastor steps to the mike and says, "Bring your burdens to the Lord church, it's altar time."

I am the first person in the aisle to walk to the altar. I hear a rush of whispers. I think they all remember my story from the newspaper and how I was falsely imprisoned for 15 years for a crime I didn't commit. The prosecutor, the doctor, and the policemen received extensive jail time for the part they played in my incarceration. Sheree turned state's evidence in the case and received 6-months probation for her testimony.

The senior ladies in white cry out and slowly stand to their feet sobbing as I pass their pew. I nod at the preacher with tear-filled eyes as he begins to pray. The people slowly join me at the altar as I drop to my knees. Pastor Worthy prays a prayer of Thanksgiving. He prays for mere existence and for our Savior's continued grace and mercy. When the prayer is over, many people come and hug me and tell me that they never stopped praying for me. I turn to go and sit, and I see Sheree. She must have been standing at the altar near me the entire time as I greeted the saints. She probably thought I was ignoring her, so she passes by me with her head down and a sad look on her face.

As she passes in front of me, I grab her hand very gently. She glances at me slightly with a tear-stained face. I have not seen or heard from her since she told me of her betrayal.

I hug her tightly and hold her close and whisper in a faint voice with plenty of emotions, "Thank-you." At that moment, I realize that I love her and she will be my wife. I don't know how I will provide for us, but I trust God.

We walk hand-in-hand as she leads me to her seat. She slowly cries and in a loud startling voice she says, "Forgive me Lord, Forgive me!" She repeats this cry over and over again. I comfort her, hugging and stating, "God hears you." The choir begins to sing, God Cares for You, and the people praise, dance, and cry.

After what seems a brief time, but is really much longer, Pastor Worthy delivers his sermon and then extends the invitation to come to Christ for anyone wanting to change their life.

This is the first Sunday I have been in church for more than 20 years, and 25 people joined and 12 people stood with me to become candidates for baptism. What a mighty blessing on my first day of real freedom.

After church many people come up to talk, shake my hand and encourage me. I am told that in the last six months the entire church had been fasting and praying for me. As I walk down the stairs, Sheree is waiting on me. She says, "It's about time, let's go home." I tell her, "I can't go home with you."

"What do you mean you can't go?"

"Sheree, I'm saved now." "I was converted in prison and God called me to preach. It's going to be hard enough to resist your body, but I know that if I go with you now, I'll be sinning and I'm trying to do the right thing. I can't do the things I used to do like have sex and not be married. Even though I've been locked up for a long time and I really want you bad, I just can't trust being alone with you in that way.

When I move in with you, I want to be your husband. I want you to be my wife, and I want to have a job where I can support you."

"I knew a guy from the old neighborhood that said he was celibate. I want to honor you in the same way. I want to remain celibate until our wedding day."

"Hey, you keep talking about marriage, but I haven't heard a proposal. "I am not going to ask you officially until I at least have a ring and a job to take care of you. So for now, think about how you will answer when I pop the question." One of the sisters told me about a shelter down the street. That's where I'm going tonight and the first thing in the morning, I will look for a job. Hopefully I will be able to find something really soon because I don't know how long I can hold out and not be with you.

15
Family Matters

It's Monday, high noon, and I have walked to a dozen businesses. People won't let your past die. Some owners told me that they did not need a thug working in their establishment. One manager told me I had a lot of nerve asking him for a job. He said, "You and your crazy Momma was stealing out of my store every time you came in here. Get off my property and don't ever come back, with your roguish self." I can't believe he remembers me after all of these years, and I don't blame him for kicking me out and calling me roguish. Me and momma used to hit his store hard for any and everything. I guess I look the same on the outside, but if he only knew, I'm truly a changed man on the inside.

Ms. Chu stopped me at the door before I could step my foot in. That woman started rattling off so many words so fast, I knew she had to be cussing me. She had a broom in her hand and was waving it at me as she shooed me away from the door. She had a frown on her face, her eyes were blood shot red and I could see the veins in her temple sticking out. Man, she remembers me too! I got out away her so fast, I almost stumbled and fell. I guess people never forget a thief, someone who took something from them or violated them.

Damn, I almost fell. My feet are tired, and I'm so hot, sweat is just rolling off of me. Forgive me Lord, but I am very frustrated. I really am ready to go back to the rooming house and just lie my weary body down, but I guess I'll try this one last business—a hardware store.

The sign reads, *"Hinton's Hardware Grand Opening in 30 days."* Would you believe this? Posted on the door is a sign that reads, "Job Openings." When I walk in the store, I ask for the manager and the attractive young lady standing at the counter directs me to the back office. As I walk back to the cramped office, I come upon a man hunched over a desk punching numbers on an adding machine. His shirt partly hangs out of his pants and his glasses sit really low on the rim of his nose. As he looks up, I introduce myself and inquire about the job postings.

He stands up, extends his hand to me and tells me his name. His hand shake is very firm and strong, even though he has a small frame and appears to be an older gentleman, maybe in his early 60's.

Mr. William Hinton is a handsome man with mingled gray hair and a wide, warm smile. He is the owner and is new to the city. But, he has only one last entry-level salesman position open.

As he begins to interview me and ask me a series of questions, I inform him of my past and my time in jail. He says he appreciates my honesty, and he tells me everyone deserves a second chance.

He can clearly see that I am inexperienced, and though he tells me that he normally does not hire people with little or no sales experience, Mr. Hinton tells me that he has a good feeling about me although he doesn't know why, he decides to give me a chance. He agrees to make me a part-time saleman with a two-week probation period to let me prove myself and see if I can do the job of making sales. As I walk out of the door, I praise God for not letting me quit before I checked out that one last spot.

The next few days go by fast. Several church members come by, and I am able to exceed my quota for the week in four days. The projected total of my sales increases every day, and I only have a couple days left before my 14-day probation ends. It happened at lunch time. I am sitting in the lounge when Marlon, another salesman, tells me a customer insists that I wait on him. It is my uncle, Sammie Lee, and he is drunk and talking loud. I whisper, "Uncle, what are you doing here? This is my job, are you crazy, uncle?" He says, "Nephew, let me holler at you over here in the corner." That man is insane, he actually wants me to hook him up with an electric saw. He says he will sneak it under his jacket. I tell him, "I am saved, Unc'.

That old life is behind me. I am a minister of the gospel. You've got to leave Uncle Sammie, before I am forced to call the police and report you for trying to steal merchandise."

Mr. Hinton comes over and asks if there is a problem. I tell him, "This is my Uncle, and he was trying to get me to help him steal. I'm showing him the front door, Sir. I think he's had a little too much to drink."

Mr. Hinton says, "Louvious Johnson, I would like to see you in my office after you escort your uncle to the door." As I walk him to the door, my uncle's mumbling, "Man, you can help a brother out, I'm family." I gently push him out the-door and tell him to please not come back here again.

I walk in the office, and I know that I have lost my job. Mr. Hinton tells me he heard my Uncle talking to a lady on the parking lot. He told the lady to let him go in. He said it would be real easy to get you to help him steal whatever he wanted. Mr. Hinton says, "Mr. Johnson, you proved to me that you could handle yourself. If a family member could not sway you to steal, I know you will be a valuable employee to our store. Let's sign a contract the first thing in the morning.

16
Godly Restraint

I can't wait to tell Sheree about the good news of my promotion. I'm now a full-time hardware salesman with benefits. Only God provided a situation that would convince Mr. Hinton that I would be a faithful and loyal employee.

Sheree and I have been seeing each other after work every since I was released. It has been really hard, but every night I have been walking back to the shelter. The smell of her perfume lingers on my clothes, and her scent is everywhere. Whenever I embrace her even with a simple touch, my whole body trembles. My palms sweat, and I start to perspire profusely. My heart races uncontrollably, and I get weak at the knees when I imagine the many times we were intimate. I feel like I'm losing control because the urges are so intense, so much so to the point where I feel like I'm about to black out. I'm constantly praying and asking God to help me fight this war between my old nature and my new nature. "Oooh it's a struggle! Her body is so soft and it's been sooo long. Help me Father!"

I have been saving most of my check every Friday, and now that I am full-time my salary will double. I tell her about the job, and she is so excited that we cry together. She tells me about how hard it was to cope after I was sentenced. She says the guilt and the mourning for our baby girl was unbearable. She was on drugs and led a very sinful life that was unspeakable. She smoked dope all day and roamed the streets at night. She went to some awful places and did some despicably shameful things that were just too painful to share. The guilt of losing the baby and deceiving the love of her life took her to depths of immorality that she never in a million years imagined.

She has been clean every since she came to visit me

in prison nearly four years ago. We are both happy and have turned our lives around with the help of our Savior. We even have nightly devotion and prayer. We are having the courtship we should have had when we first met. She tells me, "I like the person I am becoming and I love the man that you are, Lou." I tell her, "I agree with you, Baby."

17
At the Crossroads

The next week, Pastor Worthy comes by the hardware store to take me to lunch. Just think, the pastor of the church is coming to take me to lunch. I like Pastor Worthy. He is a good and decent man. He is a pillar of the community and a real family man. He's been married 50 years and has four children—all of whom are very successful. In the short time I have known him, I have watched him help people in the church and in the community. He really practices what he preaches. He extends the church to people of other faiths and has even allowed other congregations to worship in our facility when their churches were burned-out or flooded. He is truly the kind of example that I wish to follow. Man, I can't believe I'm saying something good about a preacher. I must really be saved!

I tell him my lunch hour is at noon and he tells me he will come back to talk to me. I have never in my life had a lunch date with a person to talk over anything, let alone something that might be important. I am experiencing a lot of firsts, and it feels good.

My pastor takes me to a nice, buffet-style restaurant. The variety of foods is unbelievable. I heard about this kind of place in prison, but I didn't know it could be like this. I'm used to some mystery meat, some potatoes and beans, and, every now and then, some fresh vegetables like green beans and corn. But this is like Thanksgiving, Christmas and Easter dinner rolled into one.

There are all kinds of foods—chicken, pork chops, steak, ribs, ham, turkey, and roast beef—and that's only the meats! There were so many choices—I can't make up my mind. And don't mention all the vegetables and other food items. There are all kinds of greens—collards, turnips, mustard, kale, spinach—and all kinds of salads. I see squash, green beans, okra, corn, sweet potatoes, Irish potatoes, cauliflower, broccoli, macaroni and cheese, cornbread dressing, spaghetti, and lasagna. There are so many delectable desserts, pies and breads. All kinds of cake I can choose—chocolate, strawberry shortcake, coconut, German chocolate, carrot and caramel. I think I am gonna hurt myself just looking. There is peach cobbler, sweet potato pie, lemon meringue, pecan, pumpkin, apple pie and banana pudding. There is jalapeño corn bread, hot water corn bread, rolls, garlic toast and mouth watering biscuits.

I spent the last 15 years locked up, so I am like a kid in a candy store. I watch the Pastor and take my cues from him. Of course, the preacher put some fried chicken on his plate with some of the other menu items, so I did the same thing.

"Brother Johnson, I want to hear it straight from you. I have been told that you have been called to preach." "Yes sir," I nervously say and start to explain. He stops me and says, "That's between you and God. I asked you to eat lunch with me so I can tell you that you must go to school to get educated and to learn more about the Word. I see the way you are carrying yourself at church and in the community, and I want you to prepare your first sermon in a couple of months. Is that enough time for you to prepare to come before the congregation?" I hesitantly agree, "Yeah, yeah Yes, sir. I think that ought to be enough time." "Of course, I need to look over your first sermon to make sure you're on track with doctrine according to our denomination. I will be there to mentor you all the way on your spiritual journey." "Pastor, I will be honored to be mentored by you."

"Now, son one more thing. Eat your food. I didn't bring you here for you to pile all that food on your plate and not eat. So, eat up. I know you didn't have these many choices in prison, so enjoy. Have plenty of that crispy, golden brown chicken. It's the best in town. You're a preacher now. You know they say that's what we like to eat. "Enjoy son."

I go back to work and turn up the sales. I am really happy for the first time in my life. I'm happy with me.

Unfortunately, happiness does not last long in this sinful world. You need to be ready for disappointment and distress and realize where your true happiness comes from, a relationship with Jesus Christ.

My old homeboys are waiting for me after work, Ray Ray, Fonzo, and Bleu. Yeah, those were my boys. We grew up smoking and stealing together. They are casually dressed in the latest designer clothes. The guys look a whole lot slimmer than I remember.

"Hey man, you been out for a while and you haven't been to see your boys." "Man, I'm just trying to readjust to society. I have been rehabilitated and I'm trying not to reoffend."

"What the hell?" "What's that, some new kinda prison talk?"

"Man, what's up with you?" "You working on these white folk's job and talking all funny." "If you got a new hustle, let us in on it, we game." "Lou, Man, we got some good weed." "Fonzo, give that fool some. He need to chill. Man, you with your boys." "Guys, I don't know how to break this to you, but I am a preacher." "That's what's up; you got one of the top dollar hustles. All the legal money and honey you can stand." "Man, you were always smart and quick to think of the next way to scam money."

"Look guys, I gave my life to Christ. I am not drinking, smoking or having sex." "Man you got turned out in

the joint. And what you mean, you ain't gittin' no trim?
You really dun' shot off. It's bad enough, you call yourself
preachin', but you been locked up all this time, and you ain't
runnin' at no cat? Man, please! Tell dat' to somebody else,
remember, we yo' boys."

Just then, two police cars pull up with the lights
and sirens blazing. Fonzo, Bleu and Ray Ray take off, and
one of the blue cop cars gives chase. I stand there frozen in
time looking at the red lights on the tail end of the car and
remembering all the times I ran from the police. Another
police car pulls up and the officers immediately order me
to the ground. They search me as I lie head first in the dust.
I am informed that a woman was mugged and robbed and
the perps were last seen in this area. The officers ask me,
"Which one of ya'll was involved in this incident?" I reply, "I
just got off work and I have no knowledge of a mugging or
a robbery." The officers ask the names of the guys I was talking to. In my old life you don't snitch. I am at the crossroads
of my life, the old meets the new.

A call comes in right as they ask me for my identifi-
cation. The officer glares at me. He tells me I'm lucky because I was going to go to jail, innocent or not. As both police cars speed off, I wonder how I was going to answer the
policeman's question. Would I have told them my friend's
real names? I'm glad I know now that it was nothing but
the grace of God that the police got that call, and He is the
one that kept me from going to jail.

18
Satan, Get Behind Me

It's Sunday and the day has come for my trial sermon. I have fasted, prayed and studied. I am ready to preach the Word. I am scared and my voice is strained from all the practicing, but I remember the verse... 2 Timothy 1:7: "For God has not given us a spirit of fear, but of power and of love and of a sound mind."

I become calm, make my bed at the shelter and begin my pilgrimage to the church. This is it. I hear a voice say, "Once a hustler, always a hustler." "Devil you are a lie, get behind me."

As I walked to church, I see an old classmate — Suzanne Foxx. She was one of the prettiest and finest girls in the school. She has a twin sister named Suzette equally as pretty. I almost got with Suzanne, but her mother came home early.

∾ ∾

I climbed out of her bedroom window undetected. Man that was a long, hard walk home, especially when I thought about that girl's luscious, full lips. She looks absolutely the same but better, and as she slowly walks toward me in that red, tight dress that looks like it has been air brushed on her body, my heart skips a beat. The stiletto heels show her legs that go all the way up without her thighs touching. Those legs look like they belong to an exotic pole dancer. "Hey Lou, where are you going looking, so damn fine in that suit?" "Uh, Uh, Uh, I'm heading to church." "I been partying all night," she says, "I'm about to go home, eat some breakfast and go to bed alone. I could use some company for both. Are you game?" I look at her body, and it's been sooo... damn long. I can't breathe. My mouth moves but no words come out.

Before I know it, she grabs my butt, pulls me close and kisses me smack dab in the mouth. I smell her hair—the shampoo. I know that aroma, but I can't seem to recall the name. She catches me totally off guard, and I find myself giving in to her warm embrace. I feel the Bible in my hand and step back. Way, way, way back! I try to compose myself and say, "I am preaching my first sermon" in a high pitched voice." I repeat myself, but this time with more bass in my voice and with more conviction. I say, "I have been called by God and am going to preach my first sermon." She moves closer to me with those lips and says, "If you ever get tired of playing preacher man, you can lay hands on me anytime and I'll even let you stroke me long and hard with some of that holy oil. Come see me now." She walks slowly away as I stare at her from her hair down to her shoes.

Mother Sally Lookout, a mother at the church, comes up from behind in her white suit and hat. I don't know where she came from, but I'm glad she showed up. "Thank you God for your divine intervention." She breaks that obsession just in time by saying, "Are you ready to bring the gospel, son?" I smile and say, "Yes Ma'am, I am ready!"

I notice the parking lot is full when we reach church. I walk around to the back door to Pastor Worthy's office. He greets me with a nod. He is on the phone asking someone to go down to the basement to bring in more chairs. He gets off the phone and says, "Sunday School hasn't started and we have an overflow already. Brother Lou, do you want someone to teach your Sunday School class so you can get ready for your sermon?" "No, I'm fine, Pastor. I know I'm ready. I just had a temptation that any man locked up for as long as I was probably wouldn't have passed up. But by the grace of God, I struggled through. God is Good!" "Yes, He is."

I teach my Sunday school class and am revived by the Word. I am glad I did not allow another teacher to take my class because I would have missed that spiritual opportunity.

It is 11:00 am, and the worship service starts on time. After the offering is taken and just before the praise and worship segment ends, my mind wanders and I have second thoughts about whether God really called me to preach. Maybe I was dreaming when I was in the hole. "Is all this for real? Lord, don't allow me to stand and preach today if it's not your will." At that moment, I hear Pastor Worthy call my name, and I realize he's introducing me. As I rise to my feet and slowly walk to the podium with notes and Bible in my hand, I think, "Get thee behind me Satan."

19
The Struggle Is Over

I look out at the congregation this morning, and I'm overcome with so many faces. Folding chairs are everywhere, and every pew is full with parishioners.

"Church, I won't be before you too long. I was told by Mother Lookout, 'Son, give your text, subject, three points, a couple of stories and sit your butt down.' She said, 'Don't tell everything you know in one sermon.' So I'm gonna be obedient to my elder." I'm only gonna say what God tells me to say since this is my first sermon.

How do you resist the devil when you're struggling with your old life after you have crossed over to your new life?" My subject is "Old Life, Old Nature, New Life, New Nature."

"Turn with me to Proverbs 1:7 which reads, 'The fear of the Lord is the beginning of knowledge, but fools despise wisdom and discipline.' Let us pray." After the prayer, I tell the ushers they may be seated.

What do you call a person that loves sinning? Would you call them a sinner, a thug, a heathen, a fool? I'm sure that you can think of a few more choice words, but for the sake of brevity, this list will suffice. I stand here today to tell you that I was the fool that Solomon speaks about in this passage. I didn't have God on my side and didn't know how to fear anyone let alone to fear God."

"I was a tough guy and people feared me. I had such a rep that when I was a teenager, I got into a fight at Washington Pool not far from this church."

"I was just about to dive in the pool with six of my boys. We were gonna slice as we ran toward the twelve foot deep end. Some brother stuck a stick out as I ran to the edge of the pool. I jumped over the stick and landed doing a cool swan dive in the water. Minutes later, I dragged him in the water and 'ducked' him five or six times. I pulled his head up and down in the water and didn't let him up for air. I pulled him up after I saw a few bubbles. I grabbed his head and slung it into the metal part of the lane ropes. When blood started shootin' out from his nose and ears, I tossed him back on the deck."

"I could have killed him but I didn't care. The only thing I thought was he deserved the beat down I gave him. Now, I know that it was wrong to do what I did. I could have easily communicated to him my objection to him trying to trip me with the stick.

There are quite a few young people in the audience today, and I just want to tell you that was my old nature. So I say, "Speak peace in every situation." Point #1.

Romans 12:19 says, 'Beloved, do not avenge your-selves, but rather give place to wrath; for it is written, 'Vengeance is mine, I will repay,' saith the Lord.' Instead of being violent with him, I should have spoken peace."

"I was raised in a household where violence was the order of the day. My Momma taught us that peace and good-will was for weak suckers. She was not the best role model, because she loved to fight, and she didn't fight fair. She liked to get everybody in the fray, especially her whole family. Even though my Momma had her worldly ways, I still love her, because she's Momma."

"You may have heard the old expression, 'Fruit don't fall far from the tree.' I was no exception. Momma liked to fight; I liked to fight. She was a brawler. She liked to steal; I liked to steal. She scammed folks out of their money, and I scammed folks out of their money. She was rude and had a filthy mouth; my mouth was worse."

"There's no doubt in my mind, right now, that there

may be some of you in this congregation who may have been victims of my vile actions, and I want to apologize for making offensive remarks toward homosexuals, ethnic groups, law enforcement, teachers and even the clergy.

Now, I know that it was my personal prejudices and my ignorance of so many things that drove me to have self-hate and hatred of others." "Old Nature. "Isn't it ironic that some of the very things I vilified and detested are already a part of my life, and I embrace them whole heartedly. I will be enrolling in seminary in the near future and now I know that it's alright to be smart." The congregation applauds and loudly says, "Amen."

"I didn't have any discipline or wisdom before Jesus came into my life. One morning while I was in solitary confinement for protecting myself, I was at my weakest moment. I wanted to end it all, but it was then that Jesus showed me he was always there. He spoke to my heart, and I was changed forever. This Jesus wanted me to spread His Word, and I have been speaking for Him every since."

"Church, this journey is a struggle and it hasn't been easy. In Romans 7:18-25 Paul states, 'I know that nothing good lives in me, that is, in my sinful nature. For I have the desire to do what is good, but I cannot carry it out. For what I do is not the good I want to do; no, the evil I do not want to do—this I keep on doing. Now if I do what I do not want to do, it is no longer I who do it, but it is sin living in me that does it. When I want to do good, evil is right there with me. "Old Nature." For in my inner being I delight in God's law; but I see another law at work in the members of my body, waging war against the law of my mind and making me a prisoner of the law of sin at work within my members.'

Paul goes on to say, 'What a wretched man I am! Who will rescue me from this body of death? Thanks be to God—

through Jesus Christ our Lord!"

"Right now, I continue to struggle with the lessons I learned from my Momma and how the lessons from scripture don't match up. I'm challenged everyday to do the right thing and when I pray and ask God to show me how not to yield to temptation, I gain strength in knowing that He will enable me to stand firm in His Word." So I say to you, Church, Point #2 - "Yield Not to Temptation" for yielding is sin.

"Just this morning before service, God tested me. A beautiful, desirous woman from my past interrupted me on my way to the church. She tried to entice me to go home with her and "Bible study" was not what was on her mind, if you know what I mean. She was a real temptation and I struggled mightily with resisting her. The Devil knows just what you like. Everything within my flesh, the natural man, was saying yes, yes, yes, but my new nature, the spirit man, heard James 1:12, say: 'Blessed is the man who endures temptation; for when he has been approved, he will receive the crown of life which the Lord has promised to those who love Him.'"

"Well, I'm here to tell you that if you're looking for a miracle, just look at me. I am a living testimony to the goodness and the grace of Jesus Christ. If you're tired of struggling with sin and bad habits, and you're trying to live a holy life, Point #3 - "I recommend Jesus", the habit breaker. He can change a liar, into a living epistle and a person with integrity. He can change a thief into a trustworthy trustee. He can change an accused murderer into a "Man of God, and a giver of life."

He can change a belligerent brawler into a peacemaking brother. He can turn a hustling thug into a thankful theologian. He can change a drug dependent streetwalker into a sober housewife. He even turned a wreckless reprobate like me into a Sunday School scholar with discipline and a double portion of wisdom." He gave me a New Life and a New Nature.

"I recommend you turn your life over to the man who changed my life. Jesus is His name. The man who took the spikes in his hands and feet, who wore a crown of thorns on his head, who was falsely accused, who was led from judgment hall to judgment hall, and who bled and died on the cross at Calvary for you and me. He rose from a dusty grave after 3 days and got up with all power in His hands. Will you come to Jesus, woman, man, boy and girl?"

"The doors of our Father's house are open. You can come by letter, Christian experience or as a candidate for baptism. Will you come?" Minutes pass and the church is quiet. "Church, please pray."

Suddenly, a young man at the back comes down the aisle. A family of four and a couple walking hand in hand come, then people start walking the four aisles and from the balcony. I am so taken by this amazing sight that I cry uncontrollable tears that I have been trying to hold back.

I hear a lot of commotion, clapping and loud praises. I look up from my white handkerchief already soaked with tears and sweat. I see a woman with stained clothes. Her dress is short, her heels are high and she is walking a little unsteadily. Her hair is blonde and she tosses the wig in the air. She has a pipe, but gives it to a man sitting on the pew. She is shorter now as she makes her way to the front. I guess she has taken off her shoes too. I hope she don't take off that tight, short dress. She is escorted by two ushers, and she is crying on one of their shoulders. As they walk slowly to the front, the woman starts to look familiar.

Oh my God! Praise his Holy Name! It's my Momma! I step down from the pulpit, grab her hand, and we embrace each other. The choir begins to sing, "God Is Able."

My mother shouts out, "I am tired, Lord. I can't go another step without you. I am a drunk, thieving, crackhead Ho. Please forgive me! I was a bad momma and not a good person. Help me to be the woman you want me to be." She collapses to the floor and says, "I won't get up from here until you deliver me from drugs and committing crimes. Lord, I need you right now!"

"Church, we need to pray right now for this dear sister, I mean my Momma. Mother Board, please come to the altar and assist in the prayer. The people in the church weep while I pray the prayer of salvation. I give honor to God as I try to hold it all together. I get through the prayer and ask, "Is there anyone else who wants to receive the gift of salvation?"

Thirty more people come down to the altar. At that moment, Momma does a 180 degree turn. She looked angelic, but then in a flash, her whole countenance changes. She looks totally evil like she is possessed. She is foaming at the mouth and she jumps up and runs out of the church screaming, "I'm not ready, I'm not ready!"

I am so shocked that all I can say is, "Church, please continue to pray for my Momma." The choir sings, "Shake the Devil Off," as I run out of the church after my Momma.

Pastor Worthy asks the new membership committee to come forth and they lead all the new converts to the Fellowship Hall for new member orientation. He then gives the Benediction and dismisses the congregation.

20
Victory In Christ

Months have passed and I haven't seen Momma since the day she ran out of the church. It's like she vanished into thin air. I was mere steps behind her and she was gone just like that. As far as I know, Momma is still out there in the world.

I finally proposed to Sheree and presented her with a gold wedding band. We got married at the church, and it was a beautiful ceremony. The entire church was there. Mr. Hinton was my best man, and Pastor Worthy officiated. Sheree was the most beautiful bride, and I am the most blessed man in the world. Our wedding reception was in the fellowship hall and we got lots of gifts and money. We were so surprised when my Aunt Mabel and Uncle Winton gave us a weekend honeymoon to Hot Springs, Arkansas.

Since then, we have moved into the parish house next to the church. We are talking about having a family, but we are going to take it slow. I am the assistant to Pastor Worthy. The church has doubled in size over the last two years. Our outreach, drug ministry and prison release programs have gotten national attention. Our success rate for people completing the program and changing their lives is 90.5 percent.

෴ ෴

I give all the glory to God for allowing me to go to prison so I could help people to change their lives. If He can change a hardcore thug like me, He can do it for you too, and I know that there's still hope for Momma and my family.

Don't wait! If you know that you are tired of sinning

and living a worldly life, give your life to Jesus Christ. Repeat these words.

"I know that I am a sinner and I need a Savior. I believe by faith that, Jesus Christ died on the cross for my sins. He shed his blood and He rose from the grave after three days. I repent right now and ask forgiveness for my sins. God please come into my life and show me how to live for you."

If you have repeated this sinner's prayer, you are now saved. Romans 10:9-10 says, "That if thou shall confess with thy mouth the Lord Jesus, and shall believe in thine heart that God has raised Him from the dead, thou shall be saved. For with the heart man believes unto righteousness; and with the mouth confession is made unto salvation."

Go to a local Bible teaching church and learn to grow in fellowship with other believers of the body of Christ and in the grace and the knowledge of Jesus Christ.

You can go to ***www.mshbsalvation4me.com*** to get more information on how to change over to your new Christian Life.

THE END

Not so fast, this story can't end just yet. I've told you how my son turned his life around.

I informed you about how he helped so many people change their lives by including God in their every day walk. Finally, I shared how he became a man of God. Now I need to tell you my life's story and how I got to the point where I walked the aisle of the church stripping my sinful life away. You must read my story in the next book entitled, **"Momma's Journey to Hell and Back."**

Acknowledgments

I want to thank God for planting this book in my head twenty years ago. I am grateful I was able to pour the words on to paper, resulting in the end product. I brought a skeleton to my friend, Marian Matthews Nance, who has collaborated with me in making these bones a living reality with sinew (muscle), skin, (covering) blood (life) and substance.

With grateful thanks to Dr. Rychetta Watkins who was the first to see our story and encourage us with her expertise and critical thinking in how to format and develop our novel as her apprentices in "Book Writing 101."

Much gratitude to Diann Kelley, the photographer, who shot the cover of the book and her husband, Charles, who was patient during the long, hot hours of the photo session.

With loving appreciation to my precious college sweetheart, Milton, who is the love of my life, for being patient after many months of late nights and endless drafts, enduring the trips to the library, occupying the laptop and the need for many hours of solitude.

To my son, Milton, a gift from God, thanks for all of his encouraging comments and perspectives that seemed to come at the right time.

Thanks to Sheliah Amis, my sister, who helped with the initial technical and media communications.

Thanks to Brian Montgomery, who started the book layout process and many thanks to Catrina Dean for the finishing details, layout, and downloading the final draft for publication.

Much appreciation to my nephew, Jara Tefera, for the support of accompanying me in Zion, IL to my many doctor's appointments as I battled breast cancer and his mother

Marie Owens for driving me around when I could not drive.

Thank you to my doctors especially Dr. Rosemary Miller and her husband Dr. Logan Miller and the many nurses and staff for the excellent care resulting in my being "cancer-free" as of January 3, 2013.

Glory be to "Jehovah Rapha," God, my Healer, for blessing me with His miraculous healing power.

Appendix 1

The objective of the Workbook is to transform individual readers through introspection and group verbal stimulation that will bring about insight to resolve internal and external problems.

Facilitator Guidelines

1. Group discussion will be conducted by a facilitator. The facilitator should be trained in guidance/counseling or have worked in some capacity with youth. The role of the facilitator is not to teach, but to encourage group members to join the discussion, give personal views, and achieve self- awareness from the questions.
2. The facilitator must emphasize the importance of making positive statements and being sensitive to responses made by group members as it is crucial for the overall success of the discussion.
3. The facilitator is to identify hesitant individuals and make them feel free to speak and assure them that other members of the group will be respectful and value their responses.
4. All group discussions will remain private and confidential in nature. Group members should not repeat any information shared.

Group Dynamics

The completion of questions has no time limit. The facilitator will determine how much time will be needed based on the needs of participants.

Completion of all 10 Workbook questions is optional. Be flexible and complete the sessions as directed by the group's needs. The group may decide to complete less than ten questions per chapter. Discussion of one chapter may take two weeks to complete or just one session. The facilitator and the group will determine the process.

Individual Instruction

The Workbook contains questions that can be read and completed after completion of the corresponding book chapter. The chapter questions should be completed before meeting in a group setting. The solitary time can be completed a couple of days before the group session.

The questions are not meant to be responded to quickly. Answering questions honestly will help individual growth through self-introspection resulting in a journey through the maturation process. Make or purchase a notebook to jot down your thoughts in a journal. You will be requested to write your thoughts at the conclusion of the chapter.

Chapter One - *Momma's Golden Rule*

1. The title, Momma Said, "Hit'Em Back!", is drawn from instructions given by the mother, Louvenia, to her children. Is this demand, to hit back, a common instruction given by parents? Is it helpful or harmful?

2. The code of the street was to hit back. Is this a survival tactic to coexist in some urban areas or is it advice that is one of life's lessons needed to go from childhood to adulthood?

3. Which is harder, family pressure or peer pressure? Is it more important to have a reputation and be respected or to have a reputation and be feared? How would you define "respect" and "reputation?" Compare your definitions to those found in the dictionary. How are they similar or different? Is it vital to have respect at any cost?

4. In groups of two or three, discuss whether spanking is a necessary discipline. Where do you think the line is drawn between spanking and physical abuse?

5. Do you think cursing and speaking negatively to children are forms of verbal abuse? Do you think "keeping it real" is helpful sometimes to make a point with young people? Have you ever been disrespected by someone at home or in public? How did it make you feel and how did you react?

6. Do you think a criminal record can hinder you in life, or is it important to have a criminal record to survive in the community?

7. Is your family name important, and is it crucial enough that your name causes others to fear and avoid members of your family? Is this a good thing?

8. If you are involved in a conflict, when is it okay to

walk away, avoid the conflict, or tell an authority figure what happened instead of fighting?

9. When you become a parent, what kind of discipline will you use with your children?

10. In your journal, write down a summary of Chapter One, and list three positive things that you learned from the chapter and how it made you feel about family life.

Chapter Two - *Raw Justice*

1. How important is it to fake being hard, especially around people you perceive as tough?

2. Can you be yourself and not worry about how you are perceived by others?

3. Do you think you could exist in the prison community?

4. In groups of two or three, brainstorm on what kinds of things can lead to a person being locked up?

5. Can someone that you are attracted to, or someone you're trying to get to know, influence you to do the wrong thing?

6. Is justice really blind? Is it true that people with money can hire the best defense and get off and poor people often face sentences?

7. What kind of representation do you think you will receive if you get in legal trouble?

8. Define the word public defender. Define the word attorney. Based on both definitions, discuss the difference between the two positions.

9. How can you avoid what often seems to be an unfair criminal justice system?

10. Did Lou's girlfriend, Quita, use him in order to get her desires met? After she got in trouble, why do you think she did not try to see him again?

Chapter Three - *The Straight-Laced Life*

1. How do you feel about wearing clothes (hand me downs) worn by people you do not know?

2. Do you have any experience being on public assistance (welfare, food stamps)? Is it embarrassing? Give some examples.

3. Was your father a part of your family? Was he a positive role model?

4. On a blackboard or piece of paper divided in half, write on one side the positive descriptions of your neighbors in your community and on the other side neighbors that are not favorable.

5. How would you describe your experiences with the church? With church members and/or ministers?

6. Do you think that going to church will change your life? Do you know of anyone like the character Paul Paul who was changed by attending church?

7. Are there members of your family who are so different from you that you can't see how you are related to them like the characters Aunt Mabel and Ms. Louvenia?

8. Is jealousy within the family real? Have you witnessed or experienced family jealousy in your life time?

9. Have you ever liked another family so much that you wished you were a part of their family? What specifically did you like about that family?

10. Take some quiet time and write down what you learned about yourself from reading this chapter and participating in discussion.

Chapter Four - *School Daze*

1. Would you rather be viewed by others as "cool" or "smart?"

2. What kind of "rep" do the smart (nerdy) kids have? Have you ever intentionally tried not to excel to your full potential?

3. Looking back to your last school year, can you honestly say that you did the best you could in your classes?

4. Does a parent or guardian look at your report card? Break into groups of two or three and discuss the benefits of having parental support or lack of parental support?

5. When you recall your report card, what kind of grades did you receive in school? When did your grades improve or decline?

6. Can you recall your favorite teacher? Have you had a teacher that inspired you like Mr. Stennis motivated Lou?

7. How important is education to you at this moment? Do you desire a high school diploma, a technical certificate, a 2-year degree, or a 4-year degree or higher?

8. What would you like to be doing within the next five years? What steps will you take to achieve that goal?

9. Do you have anyone in your family or neighborhood who can serve as a role model? Take a few minutes and write down questions you would ask them about how they achieved their goals.

10. Is there anyone in your family or neighborhood

whose footsteps you **do not** want to follow? Write the answer in your journal along with any insights you gained from reading this chapter.

1. Family life shapes your decisions. Describe your family life in two words and explain.

2. Much of what we learn about life, we learn from family. Break into groups of two or three and list some positive lessons and some negative lessons you've learned from your family?

3. In groups of two or three, role play a positive and a negative family situation involving a parent or parents and one or two children.

4. On a piece of paper, draw a person displaying anger on one side and a person displaying rage on the other. Using the dictionary, define the words "rage" and "anger." In your own words, describe the difference between the two.

5. How can you move from the emotion of anger to the emotion of happiness without moving into the negative emotion of rage?

6. Do you think your parents are doing a good job of raising you and your siblings? Are there things you wish they would do differently? Why?

7. Have you ever been embarrassed in public by a parent? What happened? How did it make you feel?

8. If someone starts a fight with you, do you defend yourself or do you try to reason with them?

9. After an incident blows over, do you forgive and forget or do you carry a grudge?

10. Journal your feelings on what is forgiveness and how important is it to forgive.

Chapter Six - *Stand Your Ground*

1. In prison, inmates sometimes are raped and physically attacked. Do you think that prisoners should have guaranteed rights to be protected from being harmed in jail or do you believe that they have lost their rights to such protection?

2. Are the rules for protecting yourself in jail different from what one may do on the outside?

3. Corruption in the jail appears to be ongoing. How do you think a person can maneuver through the prison system and stay out of trouble? Discuss your views.

4. Look up the word "rehabilitation." Do you think our justice system rehabilitates prison inmates? What do you think is the cause of recidivism (people returning to prison over and over again)?

5. Should inmates receive career training, anger management, and life skills to help them readjust to society when they are released from prison?

6. Solitary confinement is a dark place. How long do you think you can safely stay in a place of solitary confinement? Do you think this is cruel and inhumane punishment?

7. Do you think the criminal justice system in America deters people from committing crimes?

8. What types of crimes do you think should be punishable by imprisonment?

9. Should 17 year-old minors be tried as adults?

10. Write in your journal a summary of what you learned from reading and discussing the chapter.

Chapter Seven - *Out of the Darkness*

1. Can you experience silence for a long period of time? Do you have to interrupt the silence with music, television, or talking/texting with someone by phone?

2. Can you go to the movies or out to eat alone?

3. Do you believe a spiritual being can be present with you?

4. Have you ever experienced a spiritual emotion that has been so intense that it helped you evaluate your life?

5. Personal problems can pile up to a point where things can seem unbearable. How can you resolve your problems one by one in order to lessen your stress? Break into 3 small groups and list your answers.

6. Do you blame others for some of the problems you are presently experiencing?

7. Have you ever felt like your problems are too hard to resolve by yourself? Break into groups and discuss your answers.

8. Do you think counseling can help you to sort through personal problems and reduce the stress of trying to tackle the problems alone?

9. Do you think petitioning to a higher power for solutions to your problems is helpful?

10. Write in your journal your impressions on how to solve difficult problems, and when do you think professional help is needed?

Chapter Eight - *Say It Ain't So*

1. Is it possible to feel happy for no apparent reason?

2. Have you ever had to tell some significant other about a positive change you have in your life and you feared it would be shocking news?

3. In order to change for the better, you may have to avoid some of your family and friends. In groups of 4, role play how you might tell them that you will no longer interact with them.

4. Are there certain professions that you do not trust or want to be involved with? List the professions and why you choose to not be involved with people in those fields.

5. Define the word "depression." Have you ever been depressed or had sad feelings that you couldn't seem to shake? Describe these feelings. How did you deal with those feelings?

6. Most children do not want to disappoint their parents. Do you feel this way? Explain.

7. Have you ever been where you are torn between doing the right thing vs. being influenced to do the wrong thing?

8. Define the word "change." Is it hard to make positive changes? Discuss.

9. What are some reasons people change?

10. Write one or two paragraphs in your journal summarizing Chapter Eight.

Chapter Nine - *Forgive & Restore*

1. If you offend someone, will you apologize to them? Discuss and share your answers.

2. Have you ever experienced an enlightened moment where you reflected on negative things you've done in your life? Discuss your answers in groups of two.

3. Overall, has your life, up to this point, been the way you like it, or do you need to make changes? In your journal, list your positive behaviors and list behaviors you would like to improve.

4. Do you know someone who has been called to ministry to preach the gospel? Have you or someone you know had a negative experience with a minister?

5. Could you respect and forgive your pastor if he has been involved in an altercation, violence, abuse, theft, infidelity or any criminal act?

6. Is forgiveness optional, or is forgiveness mandatory? Discuss.

7. Can forgiving a person help to free you from the memory of what happened? Does forgiveness restore your faith in that person?

8. What are your views/thoughts about Lou's experience during the church service with the female minister and the women missionaries? Do you beleive in women preachers?

9. Have you ever cried or been emotional about something that caused you pain? Explain the incident.

10. Is it okay for a male to cry? Would you encourage the person to continue to display this emotion, or

would you think of the person in a negative way?
Write your personal answers in your journal.

Chapter Ten - *Disclosure*

1. Use the dictionary, define the word "addiction." Divide into two groups and list the different types of addiction.

2. Define the word "habit." Compare and contrast the meaning of a habit and an addiction.

3. Some behaviors can be habit-forming. Cite in your journal some habits you would like to break or you would like to positively continue. Divide into two groups and list behaviors that a person should stop doing and discuss methods that can be used to break the habit or addiction.

4. It helps to discuss a problem with a caring person or professional instead of keeping the problem bottled up. Is this a true or false statement? Discuss.

5. Have you experienced the loss of a person or the loss of a relationship? How did the loss make you feel? How did you deal with your feelings?

6. The death of a loved one is painful. Do you think the statement, "Time Heals all Wounds" can console a person?

7. Using the dictionary, define the word "mourning?" What ways do people mourn?

8. The stages of grief are: 1) Denial/Isolation 2) Anger 3) Bargaining 4) Depression 5) Acceptance. Can you explain each stage of grief? Discuss your answer.

9. Do you think you can skip any of the stages of grief and hurry the process? Discuss.

10. In your journal, write some of your impressions of Chapter ten. What new insights did you get from the discussion?

Chapter Eleven - *The Secret Is Out*

1. What does the expression, "Confession is good for the soul" mean to you? Divide into 3 groups of 3 or more and discuss.

2. Report your findings to the larger group.

3. Is it okay to keep some secrets? Do you have a right to select who you will tell the secret vs. who you will not tell?

4. What kind of secret do you think should never be hidden from a person? Why?

5. Do you believe the choice to have a baby should be discussed between two consenting adults?

6. In our society, people have babies without being married. What is your view on this matter? How do you think children of these relationships feel about their parents not choosing to get married?

7. What do you think about abstaining from sex until you get married? Is this realistic?

8. Living with a partner before marriage is common in our culture. Do you agree with this type of arrangement?

9. Do you think there is ever a time when someone should be deceived?

10. Describe how deception can be devastating? In your journal, record your impressions of Chapter Eleven.

Chapter Twelve - *Deliverance*

1. Have you ever been accused of something and were later proven innocent? How did the accusation make you feel? How did you feel about the people who believed you were guilty? Tell your story.

2. In your journal, record one of your happiest family moments? Do you have many similar experiences? If not, what do you think it would be like to have a happy family life?

3. Do you think that legal officials sometimes manipulate the justice system where innocent people like Lou are wrongfully locked up? Discuss.

4. If you were falsely accused and incarcerated illegally, could you refrain from being bitter and could you move on with your life? Discuss.

5. Do you believe one person's cries can spark an explosion of crying from hardcore men incarcerated? Discuss and divide into groups of two or three and record your answers.

6. Have you ever heard the phrase, "Music soothes the savage beast?" What does this mean to you and does it have relevance in your life?

7. Do rap, gospel, country, classical and rhythm and blues evoke a certain emotion when you hear them?

8. Divide into groups of two or three. Decide on a song that makes you feel both happy and sad. Sing the song. The other groups should evaluate whether the performance accomplished the goal of evoking emotion. Rate the performance on a scale from 1-successful, 2-neutral or 3-not successful.

9. Discuss whether question #8 related to music evoked any personal emotion. Each group member, explain your answer.

10. Write down any insight you gained from the discussion questions in Chapter 12.

Chapter Thirteen - *Free At Last!*

1. Do you think the justice system does enough to make sure that innocent people are not jailed for crimes they did not commit?

2. Fifteen years in prison as an innocent man is a long time. Do you think the justice system should pay monetary compensation in these situations?

3. If your answer is yes, how much monetary compensation should be issued? How much would be fair?

4. Lou claims he does not harbor ill feelings towards any man. Do you believe that is a realistic statement? Discuss.

5. Family members go to see their loved ones in prison. Do you think children of inmates should go to see their imprisoned family members? At what age are such visits appropriate?

6. Re-read the description of the suburban community directly outside the prison in this chapter. Compare and contrast the urban community with the suburban community. Do you think your life can be different depending on the community you live in?

7. Do you think it was smart for Lou not to have a plan as to where he would stay when he was released from jail? Discuss your answers.

8. What does the phrase, "If you fail to plan, you plan to fail" mean to you? Discuss.

9. If you were to be released from jail on a Sunday, would church be your first stop? Explain.

10. Do you think Lou's newly found faith helped to change his attitude and center him to be a calm and forgiving man? Write your answer in the journal.

Chapter Fourteen - *Answered Prayer*

1. In the book, Lou goes to the altar. What is the purpose of an altar call in a church service?

2. Have you ever stood at the altar in a church service for prayer?

3. When Sheree was at the altar, she thought Lou was ignoring her. Have you ever had a wrong impression of another person's actions? How did you feel when you realized your perception was wrong? Do you think it's important to tell the person how you felt and ask them their view about the situation?

4. Did Lou show signs of forgiveness when he grabbed Sheree's hand at the altar?

5. Define the word "empathy" using the dictionary. Role-play a situation where you may exhibit empathy.

6. Define the word "celibacy." Discuss whether this lifestyle commitment is one that you would choose.

7. Is it possible to be in jail for 15 years and wait until marriage to have sex? Discuss your answers.

8. When you move from one stage in life to another, should you have a plan as to what you will do next? Example: Lou wants to marry Sheree, but he does not have a job or a ring to present to her.

9. Define the word "plan." Discuss why it's important to have a plan of action for what you want to do in life.

10. Write down in your journal some of your plans for life after high school or the next stage in your life.

Chapter Fifteen - *Family Matters*

1. Do you know people who constantly bring up negative things you did in the past? In groups of four, role-play how you can assertively verbalize your displeasure to the person bringing up behaviors of which you are not proud.

2. Did Lou react negatively to the employers he came into contact with while looking for a job? Did he give up or push ahead?

3. Define the word "rejection" using the dictionary. How would you have handled the rejection Lou received while seeking employment?

4. Step into the employer's shoes. Can you understand why they had a negative impression of Lou?

5. After someone has served his or her time in jail, should people forget the past and give them a chance to succeed?

6. What happens to a person when he or she is not given a second chance after changing for the better?

7. What do you think of Mr. Hinton giving Lou a trial job? Is this a normal occurrence, especially for a retail merchandise store?

8. If a relative came to a store where you were working, would you help him or her to steal or would you just say no?

9. Do you think that Lou got the job at the hardware store mainly because he made the right decision not to help his uncle steal property from Mr. Hinton's store?

10. Write a short summary of Chapter Fifteen.

Chapter Sixteen - *Godly Restraint*

1. Using the dictionary, define the word "temptation." What temptation(s) do you struggle with on a day-to-day basis?

2. Have you ever done some dark, unspeakable behaviors that you are not proud of? Write your answer in your journal or share with the group.

3. How do you avoid those dark behaviors? Write your answer in your journal or share with the group.

4. Define the word "guilt" in the dictionary. Brainstorm some methods of how to get rid of guilt feelings.

5. Is it easy to share your emotions with someone you trust or a professional counselor? Discuss your views.

6. Do you think it is a good idea to take your time and develop a relationship with someone you care about like Lou did the second time with Sheree?

7. If you plan to marry one day, how long do you think is an acceptable time to date before you wed?

8. Marriage counseling is an option for prospective couples. Do you think this type of counseling is important?

9. What do you think is a good age to marry?

10. What three things have you learned from reading the chapter and participating in the group discussion? Write your answers in your journal.

Chapter Seventeen - *At the Crossroads*

1. Lou's perception of ministers changes drastically in Chapter seventeen compared to how he felt about the clergy early on in the book. What do you think are his reasons for the change of perception?

2. Why do you think Lou's luncheon invitation by Pastor Worthy brought him so much joy and excitement?

3. Can you remember the first time you went to a buffet-style restaurant? When Lou described the foods, did you have the same kind of excitement? Explain your experience.

4. Do you think a minister can learn only from the Bible or is it necessary for a minister to go to seminary to be formally educated?

5. Do you think happiness brings about success in whatever you're trying to achieve?

6. How do you battle disappointment and distress in order to bring happiness in your life? Discuss in the group and make a list of ways to deal with distress.

7. Is it difficult for your friends to accept positive changes when you have moved on and they have not? What are some possible things they can say about you?

8. Why do you think Lou did not run when the police pulled up on the scene?

9. Would you snitch on a friend if you knew they committed a crime? Why or why not?

10. Write your thoughts about Chapter Seventeen in your journal.

Chapter Eighteen - *Satan, Get Behind Me*

1. How can reading scripture help you not to be afraid? What can you do to become fearless?

2. What do you think of the scene where Lou encounters his old classmate Suzanne Foxx?

3. Why wasn't Suzanne Foxx unable to persuade Lou to go with her?

4. Do you think Mother Lookout helped Lou to avoid the temptations and advances of Suzanne Foxx?

5. How do you feel about Lou's temptation experience with Suzanne Foxx?

6. If you were in the same type of situation as Lou, do you think you could have resisted the temptation?

7. Do your behaviors mirror what you have observed from your parents?

8. Is it possible for Lou to change his life from how he was initially portrayed at the beginning of the book to how he is portrayed in Chapter Eighteen?

9. Divide into groups of three. Create an irresistible temptation scenario and role play how to resist.

10. Write your impressions of Chapter Eighteen in your journal.

Chapter Nineteen - *The Struggle Is Over*

1. Were you surprised Momma did not make a change in her life?

2. Why do you think Lou was able to change and Momma was not?

3. Can a person like Lou change for the better or does that happen only in a book?

4. Do you believe that God can change you, if you ask Him?

5. Do you think Lou was happy he waited on his plan to marry Sheree? Why do you think their relationship worked better the second time?

6. If you come up with a plan and ask God to bless it, do you think you can achieve it? How can a spiritual belief help you achieve your goals?

7. Are you struggling with your past behavior and are still yet trying to live a renewed life?

8. What do you think you need to do to stop struggling?

9. Are you ready to begin a new life? Read the last three paragraphs of Chapter Nineteen.

10. Write in your journal your decision either to retreat like Momma or surrender your life to God like Lou.

Chapter Twenty - *Victory In Christ*

1. Do you have someone in your life that slipped out of your life-- vanished?

2. Is a marriage proposal and getting married old fashioned?

3. What do you think about getting married in a church with a minister officiating?

4. A parrish house is a home that belongs to the church. Could you and your family live on the church grounds?

5. Do you want to have children? Would you like a small family or a large family with your spouse?

6. Describe the kind of parent you think you would be to your children. Would you be a role model or would you tell your children to "do as I say, not do as I do.?"

7. Should a church be concerned with ministering to members that are addicted to drugs, have mental health or physical challenges, and are financially disadvantaged?

8. Can people who have been incarcerated make a change for the better?

9. What new insights have you gained from reading this book?

10. Have you made the decision to make Jesus Christ your Savior?

Cynthia Amis Dickerson

Mrs. Dickerson is a graduate of Hamilton High School and received her B.S.ED. and M.S. from The University of Memphis. She is married to Milton L. Dickerson and resides in Memphis, TN. She has a son, Milton Amis Dickerson and a stepdaughter, Kimberly Dickerson. She is an educator and a counselor. After more than 20 years, Cynthia retired from the Total Learning Center as the Owner/Director and works in the mental health field and as a swim coach. Cynthia serves faithfully in the Usher's Ministry at Mississippi Blvd. Christian Church in Memphis, TN. Cynthia also is a grateful and blessed cancer survivor since January 2013.

Marian Matthews Nance

Mrs. Marian Nance is a graduate of Manassas High School and later received her B.B.A. from The University of Memphis and M.A. in Executive Leadership from Christian Brothers University. She is married to Herman Nance and they have three sons, Mario, Andreus and Jeremiah. She is an educator in Fire Services with the City of Memphis. Marian also is an ordained minister and serves faithfully as the Interim Pastor of St. Mary M. B. Church.